Nick Grainger
Book One
The Curse of Cleopatra

G.W. Mullins

Light Of The Moon Publishing

ISBN: 978-1-7377100-9-7

First Printing

This is a work of fiction. Names, characters, businesses, places, events and incidents are either the products of the author's imagination or used in a fictitious manner. Any resemblance to actual persons, living or dead, or actual events is purely coincidental.

Light Of The Moon Publishing has allowed this work to remain exactly as the author intended, verbatim, without editorial input.

Printed in the United States of America

For further information, on his writing, visit G.W. Mullins' web site at http://gwmullins.wix.com/books

Also Available from G.W. Mullins in Hardback, Paperback and eBook

Dream Walker
Book One:
Enter The Sandman

They say a dream is a wish, but what they forgot to mention, nightmares are dreams too.

As the city darkens and humans descend into sleep, a powerful being enters the Earth Realm. This mysterious creature, known as the Sandman, takes control of our dreams and battles for control of souls.

After a boy named Zach is taken into the other realm, he awakens to a new world filled with nightmares. He is joined by two others, Daniel and Jen, as they battle to escape the Dream World, and find their way back to reality.

Beware the Sandman is coming.

***

Rise Of The Darklighter Book One: Dark Awakening

In order to save his uncle, Malachi is forced to summon Santa Muerte, the deity of death. He offers a year of his life in exchange for help. With his soul on the line, he must do her bidding, to regain his freedom.

He quickly learns a battle is about to begin. Angels and Demons will battle for control of humanity, as the dead begin to rise. Empowered as a Dark-Lighter, Malachi must choose a side as

Armageddon begins to take place, and the last battle between good and evil begins.

Rise Of The Snow Queen
Book Two:
The War Of The
Witches

What begins as a simple, bittersweet tale about a man turned into a polar bear, grandly unfolds into a rich, mythical adventure in the best-selling book series Rise Of The Snow Queen. Based on Hans Christian Andersen's fairy tale, author G.W. Mullins expands on this story creating a new mythology that takes readers into the world of snow and ice.

In part two, the story develops long before the adventures of Gerda and Kai. It takes readers to a remote mountain village where winter claims lives at the Snow Queen's command. The story goes back to the Mirror and how it cracked, sending its shards into the world to infect the innocent. This take on the story, embarks on a much more adult tone with the mood turning rather sinister as the Snow Queen battles to obtain the mirror and rule them all. Rise Of The Snow Queen Two - War Of The Witches, is a dark fairy tale that unfolds to a conclusion you won't expect to see coming.

***Rise Of The Snow Queen
Book One:
The Polar Bear King***

The first book from the new "Rise Of The Snow Queen" four part series.

G.W. Mullins has taken timeless folklore and crafted it into a new book

series meant for adults. His updated take on the Polar Bear King and Snow Queen pay homage to the stories we all loved as children while making them more adventurous and not always allowing for a "happily ever after" ending.

The newly crowned King Valeman refuses to marry an evil witch, who reveals herself to be the infamous Snow Queen. His refusal to align himself with the dark forces causes her to cast an enchantment upon him.

Her unbreakable spell changes him beyond belief. "By light one way, by night another. Your form will change you will soon discover. By day a beast of a bear you will be, at night a man while others sleep. To break this spell you much achieve, the love of another while being a beast."

Valeman is transformed into the Polar Bear King and given seven years to find true love or the enchantment will be permanent.

***Daniel Awakens
A Ghost Story
Begins***

***Death Is Only
The Beginning***

Author G.W.
Mullins turns
back time in his
Best-Selling
"From The Dead
Of Night" book
series.

In Daniel
Awakens A Ghost
Story Begins, Mullins takes you back to the day
Daniel died. In a welcome addition to the fan
favorite series, readers will learn what happened to
Daniel.

Daniel had known his whole life something was not
right. He never connected with the woman who he
was told was his mother. As his sixteenth birthday
approached, he learned the life he had lived was
based around a hidden past. His worst suspicions
were realized when the truth of his father's affair
came to light. As Daniel ran from the house of lies,
he had no idea his young life was about to end.

Daniel awakened in the cemetery, and quickly came to learn death is only the beginning. Thrust into a world of the undead, he had no time to learn of the afterlife or the battle of good and evil. The dark ones were coming, whether he was ready or not, he would soon learn of the dark-lighters and a force of evil named Malachi.

Destined to be a leader in the fight for the balance of power, Daniel is thrust into a battle he is not ready for. He quickly learns of his abilities and the lack of experience he has to control them.   Daniel must fight to save the force of good.

***Daniel's Fate
A Ghost Story
Ends
"From the Dead
Of Night" Book
Four***

***Daniel walked
in the land of
the Dead. Now
the Dead want
him back.***

As the dark ones came for Daniel, he was forced to take refuge in the light, the last place he wanted to be. There, he was to decide his own fate. Staying in the light and ascending meant

Jen would be left defenseless. If he chose being human again, the dark ones would have the

power to take over the world. As Daniel made his decision, the dead began to rise. The dark

ones were coming forward to block the light and create hell on earth.

Death is only the beginning... From The Dead Of Night Book 4

Daniel Is Waiting A Ghost Story "From the Dead Of Night" Book One

Daniel walked in the land of the dead. Now the dead want him back!

The veil is lifted between the living and the dead as the Shadows come forward to capture him.

Daniel Stratton died in a tragic accident. His life should have been over but it was not. His spirit spent the next sixty years trying to communicate with the people who came to the cemetery where he was entombed. Then Jen came one night to the mausoleum seeking refuge from a life that was spinning out of control. There she found Daniel.

As they work together to free him from his forced confinement; they learn that the Light comes for all dead, and Daniel is forced to enter it. In his case there is no matter of choice. Inside he fights for his life and escapes but the enforcers of the light come for him. He saw seven of these shadow people within the light and each marked him. Daniel knows these Shadows will come for him. Each one of the seven will take the body of a human who had just succumbed to death turning them to Zombie like creatures to do their bidding.

Together Daniel and Jen must confront the "Shadows" so that they can survive to see another day.

***Daniel Returns
A Ghost Story
"From The
Dead Of Night"
Book Two***

Daniel walked in the land of the dead. Now the dead want him back!

The story continues where

"Daniel Is Waiting A Ghost Story" ended in a cliff hanger.

Daniel died a tragic death and should be dead. He walked in the land of the dead for too long. Then the light came for him but he refused it. He fought to escape it, but higher powers had other plans for him.

His fate was to ascend and take on the role of angel, but something went wrong. Before he could assume his role, he met Jen. When Daniel fought the light to stay with Jen, he broke the law of the dead. Within the light seven Shadow enforcers saw him. They reached out to stop him and in doing so marked him. When Daniel escaped, he knew the seven would come for him.

The forces of good and evil watch to see who can claim Daniel in the end and control the ultimate power that is growing within him.

Messages From The Other Side Stories of the Dead, Their Communication, and Unfinished Business

Best-selling author G.W. Mullins shares his personal journey towards understanding death, the afterlife and communication with spirits of loved ones who have passed over. In "Messages From The Other Side Stories of the Dead, Their Communication, and Unfinished Business," Mullins tells of dealing with the grief of his mother passing and the reassurance of an after death communication that totally changed his outlook towards death and grief.

This book not only tells of Mullins' personal journey into understanding but also guides others to understand why we receive communications and the signs to look for. Mullins also explores visitation dreams and tells of his own personal experience in the area and shares the stories of others who have had similar experiences.

This book highlights the author's personal journey in an exploration for knowledge, and his understanding, without question, there is life after death. Mullins invites you to join him on this journey through life and death.

***Vengeance
A Paranormal
Murder Mystery***

*"Mystery, Murder, Paranormal Events, and a story that leaves you guessing as the bodies stack up."
– Matthew Trent
OutLoud
Magazine*

After the death of her father, Danni starts a new life in a seaside town in New York where she and her mother move into a strange Gothic house with a terrible history. From the moment Danni gets there, she feels she is being watched. She is sure they are not alone in the house.

As Danni learns of her new home, she is told of a past resident who fell to her death on the nearby cliffs at the same time that her teenaged daughter, Elizabeth, disappeared.

Elizabeth's spirit, appears to Danni and claims that her mother's death was a murder, not suicide and asks for Danni's help in bringing the dangerous killer to justice.

The mystery unfolds as Danni enlists the help of the hunky new friend she has made named Joe. A romance develops between them, but does Joe know more about the murder and disappearance than he is letting on? Will Danni live to solve the murder?

Nick Grainger And The Curse Of Cleopatra

Other titles available from G.W. Mullins include:

Timeless - An Adult Paranormal Romance Novel

The Native American Story Book Volume 1-5-
Stories Of The American Indians For Children

Walking With Spirits Volumes 1-6 Native American
Myths, Legends, And Folklore

The Native American Cookbook

Star People, Sky Gods And Other Tales of The
Native American Indians

Cherokee A Collection of American Indian Legends,
Stories And Fables

**Included at the end of this book, are the first two
chapters of G.W. Mullins' Best-Selling title
Rise Of The Dark Lighter Book One –
Dark Awakening**

For Clarence

"everything has its balance—in madness is much wisdom, and in wisdom much madness."
— **H. Rider Haggard, Cleopatra**

Before

The sounds of fighting filled the area all about her, as Cleopatra lifted herself from her golden throne. As she paced, her mind raced, as she feverishly sought a way out of her impending doom.

As she turned on her heels, she spoke aloud. "I will not give in to the Romans. I will not be a prisoner to be paraded around by Octavian as a trophy of his conquest. I would rather die before this dishonor."

She threw her head back as she studied the walls of her chamber. There was no escape for her this time. As she contemplated her final moves, she thought back on her life. Cleopatra had been blood-thirsty in her acquisition of royalty. Not much more than a murderer, she had been prepared to remove anyone who stood in her way.

Moving back to her throne, she slid comfortably to her seat and called for her servants. Two women entered the chamber, they knew why they were there, and what Cleopatra had asked for. As they approached, the older of the two kneeled at her feet, and held out the woven basket to her.

"Is it what I asked for?" Cleopatra asked.

"Yes, my queen. An asp, as poisonous as any that could be found." The older woman replied.

"Yes, but how do I know this is true. I would not dare allow this creature to bite me and its promise not be fulfilled." Cleopatra looked down at the kneeling woman, with a crazed look on her face. "You will show me of its power, put your hand in the basket."

"No, my queen, I beg of you!" The woman cried out.

"How dare you tell me no. I am the Queen of Egypt and until I depart this world, you will obey me."

Cleopatra rose to her feet and pulled out a knife from her breastplate. As she lunged forward, she found her mark in the woman's neck, slicing her carotid artery. Blood flew forth in waves as it coated the steps leading from the throne. As the basket fell in front of the woman, Cleopatra grasped it in her hands.

As she turned around, she looked at the young girl servant. "So, my pretty one, it seems you have two options, die at my hands, or gently fade away from the poison of the asp. You decide."

The girl shook in fear as she studied the room. She had no way out. As she looked into the desperate eyes of her Queen, she decided her fate. She reached out her arm as she drew closer to Cleopatra. Without saying a word, she offered her life in the test if the creatures poison.

"I do this because I have no other choice. It is not because I am loyal to you." The girl's voice echoed her disgust.

"Save your breath, I do not care what you think. In the end, you will serve your queen whether you like it or not."

As the girl's arm reached the basket, Cleopatra released the rope that kept it closed. Then taking hold of the girl, she forced her hand inside. The creature, already enraged buy the constant movement of the basket, struck hard driving its venom deep into her skin.

As the girl fell to the floor she stared in the eyes of her murderer. "You may not pay in this life. But in the next, I wish you nothing but pain and torment." As the girl's voice trailed off, she slowly fell to her side. The poison had worked, she was dead.

Cleopatra walked over and looked at the girl as her lifeless body lay on the floor. As she kneeled beside her, Cleopatra took a deep breath. A tear ran from her eye as she stroked the girl's hair. "You were such a beautiful young thing. I was as beautiful as you once."

As cleopatra pulled the girl into her lap, her demeanor changed. She seemed motherly and caring. Her mind raced from state to state. She was unstable, perhaps bordering on psychotic. She cried as she held the girl. Fear gripped her as she realized there was little time left.

Turning to the older woman, she studied her. "If I changed your clothing, and applied makeup to your face, you could be made to look as I do." She talked to herself as she prepared the body of the older woman. Dressing her in fine clothing and changing her hair, she created a very good likeness of herself.

Grabbing ahold of the woman, she dragged her lifeless body to a bench a few feet from her. "I may have to allow you to impersonate me, but I will be damned if you do it on my throne." Then she pulled the younger girl to the side of the seat and positioned her alongside. She laughed out loud as she studied the scene she had set. "A murder suicide if I have ever seen one." She said as she placed the knife, she had used earlier beside the girl.

As she turned to leave the chamber, she moved behind her throne, and reached to the back where a hidden compartment was. Inside she pulled out a set of colored crystals. Each different in color and size, they all had a particular purpose.

Cleopatra moved quickly through the complex, avoiding all that might see her. As she entered the final chamber, in a darkened corner was a table in front of a large obelisk. She moved quickly, as she laid the crystals out on the table and began to arrange them in a particular order.

As she placed the last red colored crystal in position, a light began to emit from inside the pyramid shaped opening. A gateway of light formed in the front of the structure. Then a light blasted forward in a blinding beam, as it quieted and Cleopatra moved forward. She turned to look around her as she prepared to enter. "Until I return." She said laughing as she climbed through the opening and was gone as the light disappeared.

Chapter One: Egypt Present Day

Nick couldn't help the smile on his face as he approached the great pyramid. He had dreamed of this his whole life. He had never believed he would be able to explore this, or any other ancient ruin, but when his professor offered the opportunity to go to Egypt, he knew he could not refuse.

Professor Newton was a well-known archeologist, and very respected in his field. He had been trying for years to arrange an expedition of ruins in Egypt, but with all the unrest in the area, his university refused to allow the trip. When the climate had settled and seemed to be safer, he pitched his idea again. This time, the committee who had rejected him so many times, had no choice to approve his request and allow for two of his top students to travel with him as well.

The professor chose Nick Grainger, his top student as his first choice. Nick had excelled at everything since he entered the university at the age of 16. He had already completed a degree in science when he chose to continue in the field of Archeology on his 20th birthday. Nick was probably one of the brightest students in the whole school, but lacked direction.

The second student the professor chose was Emma Blunt. Emma was 19, and a very pretty girl and a brilliant student. She was enthusiastic in her studies, and the runner up student in the department. She always seemed to come in second to Nick, and everyone was beginning to notice her resentment to him. The professor was hoping the expedition would somehow bring a little peace between them.

As Nick studied the stones that made up the giant pyramid, he did not notice that the professor and Emma had come up behind him. "Impressive, isn't it?" The professor asked.

"Amazing!" Nick replied. "I am overwhelmed. I never thought it would be so close I could touch it."

The professor laughed, "Then touch it and get a feel of the last ancient wonder of the world, the Great Pyramid of Giza." They all stepped back as they looked to the top of the pyramid in amazement of its size.

"What's on the agenda for the day professor?" Emma said catching her breath.

"I thought today we would tour a few places and get a feel for the Ancients. Then tomorrow we begin exploring a new hidden chamber that was discovered just before we came here."

As they moved inside the pyramid, the professor led them on a guided tour. Nick was in awe of the sites and the antiquity of everything he saw. His mind raced to try to understand why the place was built and how someone in ancient Egypt designed it. In his mind, he was sure there was some alien history behind everything. He had seen a television show that said the pyramid was a part of a network of power stations. He liked this idea.

The group moved on from location to location, seeing the tombs that had been opened to the public as well as some areas that were not. The whole experience was so much to take in, that when they arrived back at their hotel, everyone was exhausted. Going their separate ways, they all settled in for the night.

As the night grew later, Nick ventured out to the vending area and ice machine, trying to get something cold to drink. As he rounded the corner, he saw her standing there. He studied Emma, she was beautiful, but so out of his league. He thought about it, but knew they had been at each other's throats since they met.

Emma studied the options in the machine. She wanted chocolate, but the machine was loaded with things she did not know or want to know of. She turned to the side and looked at the next machine, she caught a glimpse of Nick. She had always had a weird attraction to him, even though on most days she could not stand him. She didn't know how to explained it, but he was cute in his own nerdy way. And for her that worked.

Nick cleared his throat, as he prepared to approach her. "Anything good in there?" He asked as he stared over her shoulder.

"I have no idea; I don't recognize any of this." Emma replied. "I guess I am out of luck, because there is no way I am venturing out into the streets at night around here."

"I'll go for you. What do you want?" He asked.

"I just wanted chocolate, but it's no big deal."

"I'll get it for you." Nick said as he turned to walk away.

"Why would you do anything for me? I thought you hated me." She questioned him.

"Well, maybe because, we are here for the next few weeks and we need to find a way to get along. Also, I agree, you should not be out on those streets at night. So, I will go for you."

"Thanks Nick." She said as he walked away.

Later that night, Emma sat in her room trying to get the internet to work with the poor reception of the hotel. As she was about to give up and put it aside, she heard a knock at her door.

Opening it, she saw a bag on the floor, as she looked in, there were several candy bars, of all different types inside. Nick had fulfilled his promise. She saw the figure of a boy rounding the corner as she looked for him. If he had stayed, he would have seen the huge smile on her face. Peace had been found.

As Emma sat upon her bed, she pulled out her cell phone and looked for Nick's number. She was sure she had it, since all the classmates had shared numbers earlier that year. Then she found it on the list. She pulled up the text screen and started to type. Mid-sentence she stopped. No, she thought, there was a better way. She searched through until she found an emoji with a huge smiling face. She decided it was perfect, and it was sent. She sat back against a pillow on her bed and unwrapped some of her chocolate and smiled.

Chapter Two: Through the Gate

The hot sun beat down on Nick, as he walked through the sands of the Valley of the Kings. He felt the moisture on the back of his head, as it ran down his neck. Reaching the dig site, he took off his hat and poured water from his canteen over his head, in an attempt to relieve the heat. His attempt was short lived as the water evaporated shortly after hitting his skin.

As he turned to look for the professor, a scream came from the distance. It was Emma. Nick did not know if she was in danger or excited, but still he rushed to her. Her screams got louder as he headed away from the dig site to a hidden place in the distance.

As he arrived, he found Emma and the professor outside a doorway, that was hidden until that day. Stepping close to the opening, he scanned the room, taking in every bit of the treasure it held inside. He had never seen anything like this in person. His mind raced to identify who it had once belonged to.

"What do you think my boy?" The professor asked,

"It is beyond my wildest dreams. How did you find it?" Nick asked, trying to contain his excitement.

"One of the workers tripped over a rock that is the top of the doorway. He told the professor, and we came and dug out the opening." Emma replied.

"Have you gone further in the doorway?" Nick could not contain himself.

"No, we were waiting for you, so we could do this together." The professor spoke, as he motioned for the two to enter.

As they looked around, each was in awe of the state of the chamber. Everything was as it would have been the day it was sealed. Nick walked the perimeter of the room looking at the hieroglyphs. He had to know whose tomb this was. As he passed by the last wall, he saw it out of the corner of his eye. The symbols for Cleopatra.

"No…this can't be. No one has ever found reference to her tomb. Can this be it?" Nick said under his breath.

"What are you talking about boy? Did you say Cleopatra?" The professor asked.

"Yes, here on the wall, these are her symbols. The hieroglyphs, talk of the Queen and her death. This is her final resting place." Nick fell to his knees as he read the line, and realized what they had found.

"What do we do now? Do we leave to tell someone? How does this work?" Emma was full of questions, as she tried to keep her long blond hair from falling into her face, as she stared at the wall.

"We will contact the authorities in time. For now, I want to look around, before they usher us out and we are not allowed back." The professor insisted.

Nick studied the chamber watching for weaknesses in the structure. He was curious how a place buried under the sands could have held up for so long without caving in. He walked from corner to corner, until he was sure the place would not collapse and kill them.

As he walked back to the rear of the chamber, he saw it there, braced against the wall. It was a large obelisk black in color, that had an odd shine on the surface. As he studied it, he ran his fingers over the surface. It was smooth, like it had been coated with a substance he did not recognize. The object almost looked alien in origin.

In front was a table with crystals laid out in an order. They were all different colors, and were space equally apart like a pattern with one open space. On the edge of the table was one red crystal that had not been placed in its opening. Nick stared at the crystals. He had the urge to move the red one into place but knew he should not touch the relics.

"Professor, there is a weird looking obelisk back here." Nick called out.

"What do you mean by weird." He called back.

"I mean, like one of these things is not like the others weird."

"Nick don't be stupid; how can something not belong…. here?" Emma's words trailed off as she approached the crystals.

"This can't be right. These aren't from Ancient Egypt. This looks like some kind of device, and the obelisk has a doorway. See, look at the markings, this is sure to open somehow." As the professor spoke, he ran a finger over what felt like a button, and the closed covering retracted to show the inside.

They stared into the darkness of the object, as Nick fumbled for his flashlight. Inside, his beam showed a void, larger than the space should have had. It was like a room within another dimension. The space was a void, only containing a view screen and another table of crystals.

"What do we do now?" Nick asked feverishly.

"Can we touch it?" Emma asked.

"I have no idea." The professor answered as he stared at the opening.

Nick reached forward to put his hand inside the obelisk, as a sound came from behind. The three jumped as if they had been hit by electricity. Behind them was Shabakaa, worker on the dig. He stepped inside the chamber as his eyes lit up in amazement.

"Look at what you have found." He spoke.

"Yes, wonderful things. Can you believe it?" Nick responded as he stepped backwards, and bumped the table of crystals.

As he turned, Nick saw the red crystal roll off the back of the table and land in the empty spot. Suddenly, the crystals began to glow and their light grew stronger until it illuminated the inside of the chamber. As the professor and Emma turned and looked at the lights, the obelisk began to light from within.

They turned to look at each other in disbelief as a bright blue wave of light shot forward and enveloped them all. The ground began to shake like an earthquake, as the four were dragged into the gateway. The light grew in intensity, as the opening to the chamber became enclosed in a slide of sand and rock. From the outside, no one would have known it was ever there. No one was left on the inside to tell the story.

Chapter Three: Shabakaa, I Get the Feeling We Are
Not in Egypt Anymore

"Nick, what the hell did you do?" Emma's words became stretched and mechanical as she disappeared into the light.

A long shaft of light formed as they were drug into a wormhole through time and space. Nick tried to move as his body became transparent. He had no feeling in his legs or arms, except the sensation of being cold as he watched a frosty ice begin to shape around him. He had no concept of what was happening, he just wished it to be over.

As suddenly as it began, the light changed and the four were shot out the other side of the wormhole. They were thrown from the gate one at a time landing hard on the ground in front of what looked like another obelisk.

Nick lay on his back trying to regain the feeling in his body. He hoped the feeling was not permanent, and that if they had to go back through again, it would not be as hard. He sat up and looked around. Shaking his head, he knew this place was not right.

Nick cleared his throat and tried to speak. "Is everyone alright?"

"Yeah, I guess so, being you almost got us killed." Emma raged as she took to her feet, almost falling down.

Shabakaa grabbed her arms as Emma tried to charge at Nick. She was out of control and not thinking straight. The professor moved between them and created a wall. He knew he had to put an end to this.

"Emma, calm down." The professor screamed. "This is no more Nick's fault as anyone else's. He had no way of controlling what happened. We have to be calm and keep our heads and figure out where we are."

"Yeah, where the hell are we?" Shabakaa asked.

"I'd say in another place and time entirely." Nick said as he pointed to the storm moving towards them."

As the group turned to look at the ice storm, the ground in front of them began to freeze. A frozen rain came from the sky as they struggled to look for shelter. The wind stung their eyes, as it whipped sleet and snow in freezing rain in their direction.

On the side of the road, just to the left of them, looked like a house with a light on. They ran for the front door trying to escape the sting of the ice pellets that shot like frozen projectiles into their skin.

As they reached the door, Nick turned the knob and they fell inside as the frost that was coating the ground came just behind their feet. The professor slammed the door, just as the icy coating came up the front steps.

"What the hell was that? I have been in some bad storms, but nothing like the Ice Age that is happening out there." Emma said as she struggled to free her lungs of the cold air.

"That's just it, we are in an Ice Age. It just started here weeks ago, and has been moving continent to continent. Now it has come to us." The voice came from behind.

Nick scrambled to his feet to see who was speaking. As he walked over to the light in the living room, he looked up to see a copy of himself standing there. This version was not the same Nick Grainger that left Egypt, this was an older Nick who had suffered through the gateway many years before. His clothes were torn, his body battered. He had suffered in his time of gate travel.

As the others gathered around, they looked at the two versions of Nick. As Emma moved into the light, The older Nick stared at her. He was fixated on her face. His expression told on him. There was grief within him.

"Hello Emma." The older Nick spoke nervously.

"Hello. I don't want to be rude, but why are you looking at me that way?" She asked.

"I am sorry, I have been alone for a while now, and I have forgotten my manners. It's just that in my trip through the gate, you died two years ago."

"How long ago did you leave your world?" The professor asked.

"I have been travelling for about 8 years now. The last couple of years I have been alone. Many of the worlds I have traveled to, have been baren wastelands, except this one. There were people here, before the storm came."

"What happened to the others you traveled with?" Emma asked.

"They died, one by one, on the worlds where there were people. There were sicknesses and conditions we were not ready for. How could we be ready? We traveled by accident on my world. If I hadn't activated the obelisk, they'd all be alive, and I would be at home now." He hung his head and turned away from them.

"Nick, it was not your fault, I am sure it was an accident, just as when we went through the gate." Emma spoke to him as she turned her eyes to her own Nick, in a way trying to apologize to him.

Nick acknowledged her gesture by shaking his head. He did not hold a grudge, but he did feel responsible for what had happened. Deep inside, he was more concerned with what had happened to his counterpart. If everyone who left with the other Nick had died, what was his own fate.

Emma stared at the other Nick. She felt so bad for him, but she felt there was more to his story. As he sat at a table near the roaring fireplace, she walked up behind him. Placing a hand on his shoulder, she tried to give him some comfort. As her fingers touched him, he looked up in a familiar loving way. Emma knew there was something he needed to say.

"How did your Emma die?" She spoke softly still holding onto him.

"We went to a planet, that was very much like a place on my planet called Egypt."

"We have that place on my world too." Emma interrupted him.

"Well in this other world, the gods who lived in the past, had escaped and set up a new life. We did not know this when we went through the gate. They were evil, vile and deadly. They live off the lifeforce of others. We learned that quickly and Emma was robbed of her life by one of them. We had only been married a few weeks when we went through the gate."

The older Nick lowered his head to hide the tears running down his face. The others looked on as Emma embraced him. She held on, even though the pain inside her was growing out of control. She feared her own death. She did not want the same thing happening to her group of travelers.

Chapter Four: Beware the Jabberwock

Emma turned away from the older Version of Nick and walked towards her group. As she moved, she wiped away her tears with a quick movement of her had. Her ego did not allow her to show such emotions to a group of people she sought respect from.

Walking towards the door, she came up beside Nick and put her hand on his back. As he turned, she smiled at him. Deep down inside, she knew she had been wrong to have treated him so roughly. She had to make it right.

"Look, I will be the first to admit I am wrong. With you, I have made mistakes, perhaps out of frustration, at times when I have to fight twice as hard to get the same respect you get. That is not your fault and I apologize for treating you badly."

"Thank-you. I appreciate that more than you will know. …And I never thought you ever came in behind me, I always looked at you as an equal. So, in another universe, we were married. Crazy huh?" Nick laughed.

"Stranger things have happened. In another universe, I am now dead. So, I am trying not to get too into the idea." Emma choked on her words.

"I won't let that happen. I will do whatever it takes to protect you." Nick insisted.

"Yeah, I bet he would have said the same thing in your place. Sadly, it means little. She is dead and he is here alone." Emma tried to fight back her emotions, but was losing the battle.

"Ok Nick, you survived, and obviously you know more than I do, about how to go through the gateway. How do we get home?" The professor asked.

"Don't you get it? You can't go home. I have been through hundreds of worlds, and jumped time and again through the gate. I could never control where I ended up. I can show you how to activate the gate, but targeting a place and time is impossible without the knowledge of the Ancient Egyptians who created it." The older version of Nick sat with his hands to his head. He was tired and his days of fighting were over.

"Ok, then show us what you know and we will go on our way." Nick insisted.

"You will die, just as they did. Just stay here with me and we will ride this out together."

"You will die here. This storm is going to send this planet into the next ice age. If you do not leave, you will freeze to death." Emma yelled at him hoping he would remember his wife. But her words fell on deaf ears. He was giving up.

The older Nick knew he had no chance making them stay, and agreed to give them a crash course in using the gate. He told them of every experience he had and ways to exit the gate more alert. Then he gave Nick the control crystal he had carried with him since the beginning.

"Keep this, it is like a key. No matter what world you end up on, this will activate your obelisk gate. If you find the Ancients, maybe they can tell you how to gate home. Never worked for me, but maybe you will have better luck." The older Nick said as he handed over the red crystal.

"Now I guess the bigger issue is, how to get from here to that obelisk without freezing to death." Nick said as he staired out the window which was quickly frosting over.

"I saw we load ourselves with coats and run like hell." The professor said as the older Nick brought in an armful of heavy winter coats.

"Nick, please come with us. Don't stay here alone." Emma pleaded with him.

As they dressed and headed out the door, Nick said goodbye to his older self. He wished there was a way to get him to come with them. As they hit the ground running, Nick held the crystal in his hand and was prepared to hit the table, as soon as he was within reach.

From behind they heard a scream calling out to them. As they turned, they saw the older Nick running in their direction. While Nick was placing the crystal onto the table, he heard one last scream. As he turned, he saw the large shard of ice falling from the overhead powerline. It cut through the older Nick's body. He was frozen solid before he hit the ground.

With the gateway opened, the group jumped in and flew through the wormhole. There was no time to grieve the lost. The time in the gate lasted less this time than the first, and when the light from the other end showed, they were all thrown free.

"Is everyone OK?" Nick yelled out.

"Yes, we all made it." Shabakaa replied.

"Not all of us." Emma said as she thought about the older Nick.

"I know Emma, I wish it could have happened differently. I just don't know how we could have changed things." The professor tried to calm her.

As they spoke, a loud roaring noise, came from out of the distance. It was like nothing they had ever heard before, but they were sure it was enormous. Loud footsteps pounded the ground and the noise got closer.

As they looked around, they saw the ruins in the distance. It was an abandoned structure, much like you would have seen from an ancient time. It was in advanced decay, but there were large stone halls leading in, that they might be able to use to hide.

They ran for the opening and stopped short just inside the stone courtyard. There on a wall, someone had painted in large letters, 'Beware the Jabberwock." Nick stared at the words for a moment and wondered who had been there ahead of them. Had another version of them already been to this place?

As the large creature came into view, Emma grabbed Nick's arm and dragged him forward. The creature ran forward quickly, as they flew into the covered space. Nick studied the walls as the creature tried to force its way inside. Someone else had been here before, there was more writing on the walls. He was sure this place was dangerous. They had to leave.

Chapter Five: Living in the Land of the Lost

"What the hell was that?" Emma screamed.

"Something big!" Shabakaa yelled back as he landed on the cement floor.

"Big is right." The professor said trying to find his words. "That is a dinosaur."

"No way, they don't exist anymore." Shabakaa insisted.

"Not on our Earth, or in our time. We are on a different planet in a different time space. Who knows if they even had an Ice Age."

Nick studied the wall and looked at all the words scratched on it. He was unsure who had written it, but someone, possibly human, had been there. He tried to make sense of it all. The person who wrote the messages, seemed to be slipping in and out of sanity. The writings were unintelligible at times.

"Professor, there was someone here before us, and I would say they were terrified for their life. Look at the wall, and I think you will understand." Nick barely finished his words as the large dinosaur came to the opening of the doorway.

Nick pulled Emma back, as the creature tore at the opening with its large teeth. With every lunge, the dinosaur's teeth came in closer. As the group moved backward, they realized there was only one way to go and it was not back the way they came.

Nick grabbed at the professor to try to get him moving, but he pulled away. "I have to read this; it may be important to our survival."

"No, we have to leave, before that thing tears open the stones enough to get to us. I am sorry professor, but we have to go into the tunnels." Nick screamed

"Ok, you're right. Let's go. I just hope that thing doesn't have any friends deeper into the complex." The professor said as he began to run.

As the group fled for their lives, they did not look back at the creature, or see all of the writing on the wall. They were on Earth after all, just in a time before the Ice Age. A time when an ancient alien race had once ruled, and caused their own nuclear destruction.

As they traveled through the vast corridor, they ran into a maze of tunnels and rooms hidden by doors. There was no way of knowing where to go. The doors were marked in a language that was mostly symbols. Not like hieroglyphs, but more like computerized modern images.

Nick turned to the professor. "What do you make of this? The outer area had writing in English and here is an alien looking glyph system"

"There was always a theory that life on earth did not start with humans as we know them. It was theorized that we might have come from a superior race that killed itself off. Maybe this world started the same way."

"That sounds like something from some show about ancient aliens or something. Sounds like a nutcase theory." Shabakaa responded.

"You want to explain this then?" Nick jumped at him.

"No, I have no…idea. I just want to go home." He responded.

"We all want to go home. I just don't know how to do that. I just know how to use this crystal, but to do that, we would need an obelisk and a dialing table. Right now, we have neither." Nick said, as he began to walk towards a door in front of him.

He studied the door and looked for a way to make it open. There was no handle, and no means of physically opening it. Then he saw on the wall beside the door, there was a shaped indention that resembled the bottom of the crystal. Holding the crystal up to the opening, he rotated it until the shape matched and then inserted it.

As the crystal slid perfectly into place, the area around the door lit up with a red color much like the crystal. A creaking sound came from the door, as it drug itself back into the wall and opened. Nick looked at the professor and they both shook their heads.

"I would say we have a functioning key." Nick said as he swallowed hard.

"Yeah, but a key to what?" Emma question.

"One way to find out, let's go inside." Shabakaa said as he pushed past the others.

The professor moved forward and caught Shabakaa by his shirt. "Nope, this is not your find. Nick is leading this expedition."

Nick stepped through and scanned to see if it was safe. As he looked around, he saw what had once been a laboratory. He searched for a way to light the room, since there was no natural light source. He reached in his pocket and retrieved his cell phone and used it as a light as he scanned the tables.

Just to the left of the door was a pad that was dimly lit as if it was running in sleep mode. As he approached, he saw that there was a handprint on the surface. An outline that suggested you would place your palm there to activate the device.

He raised his hand and began to place it towards the pad, as he studied the shape of the original users. Their hands were more reptile in shape, with longer nails at the end. These were not humans. This confused him even more, since the writing in the outer corridor was written in English.

Nick swallowed hard, as he pushed his hand towards the surface. In his mind he repeated to himself, that he had no choice. As his fingers made contact with the outline of the alien hand, the lights in the laboratory began to increase, the longer he held his hand there.

Nick turned to the door and looked at the others and got ready to tell them to come forward, as Emma began to scream. A look of confusion crossed his face as he spun around on his heels, prepared to see an attacker. Instead, the sight in front of him chilled him to his bones. His heart raced as he tried to move, but he was paralyzed.

Chapter Six: Ancient Aliens Did Exist

Nick lifted his eyes, as he staired into the row of glass chambers before him. They were filled with a blueish green fluid. Each one, still as intact as the day they were created. Each holding a secret of the death it possessed. Nick felt a lump rising in his throat as he forced his feet to move.

The others came through the door, following in his tracks. Emma looked into the first chamber which stood before her. A lifeless human form floated there, as if frozen in some state of suspended animation. She looked deep into the form and wondered if it had ever been alive, or was it just a leftover from some form of creation.

"Professor, are they human, or just some freak experiment?" Emma asked, as she felt a shiver run down her spine.

"I believe they were an experiment that went wrong. Perhaps, they never lived, they were grown here to possibly start life." He explained. "Maybe this Earth has not had its Ice Age yet, and if that is so, maybe these were meant to be the human replacements for our dinosaur friends out there. If our earth had a previous advanced civilization, maybe they created our species in this fashion. I guess we will never know."

"I think you do know. You do not wish to believe." A voice came from deep within the chambers.

"Who's there. Show yourself." Nick called out.

From behind a wall of glass and metal, a figure appeared. He came out slowly and moved in an odd way. As he walked, his body bobbed back and forth, as if he was dragging his legs. Coming fully into the light, they could see his reptilian form. Emma stepped back behind the professor, terrified by the sight of him.

"Do not be afraid, I am not here to harm you. My name is Inak. I am a traveler such as yourselves. I came from the future of this world." He explained. "My people face destruction, if I do not reset the course of this world. My ancestors here are barbaric and uncivilized. I have to find a way to educate them and stop this event from happening."

"Why are there humans in these chambers?" Emma blurted out.

"They were a failed experiment by a fellow traveler. He believed that a new race on this planet could be a...." His voice trailed off.

"A what...maybe a source of slave labor?" The professor said angrily."

"That, among other things. We also needed a source of food. It was hoped, they could serve as both as they multiplied and grew in numbers." Inak turned away from them, ashamed of his words.

"You would have eaten them. How could you do that?" Emma yelled at him.

"We all have to survive. I personally found it unappealing. I did not participate in my fellow scientist's practices. I still do not believe in it. Now, he is dead, and I am the only one here to continue trying to correct other's mistakes." Inak tried to reassure them.

"Why should we believe you?" Nick asked.

"You may believe what you will. I have no reason to lie to you. I am not here to interact with you at all. I have work to do, and as it would seem, I am the only one to do it now."

"What happened to the other scientist?" Nick became curious.

"He died here in this lab. It seemed that while he was working, my people of this time found a way in. When they saw he was trying to create life, they killed him. They thought he was defying the laws of the Great Ones, our ancestors. They came at him in a group, and ripped the outer skin from his body. I was out surveying the land, and when I came back, I found the lab all but torn apart, and Sceno was murdered by his own people." Inak stopped speaking as he looked to the place where he had found the body.

"I am sorry to hear what happened to your friend." Nick said respectfully.

"What is…a friend?" Inak asked.

"Someone you know and care about. One who you share things with." Emma answered him.

"Then he was not my friend." Inak insisted. "He was someone I traveled with. My people do not associate in this way. We have mates that we take for life, but we are not friends with others. We do communicate and interact. Nothing more." He replied.

"That's sad." Emma said under her breath.

"Not sad, not anything. It is just the way of my people. We do not miss what we do not know. This is our life."

"If your people tore this place apart, why does it look so clean now?" Shabakaa asked.

"I repaired what they destroyed and removed the remains. I even continued the experiment to create life. My results were no better than Sceno. The test subjects grew to a certain point in life, and then faced degradation at a molecular level. Since we had no reference point, there was no way to stabilize the growth pattern. We were so close. I was sure this last attempt would work." He looked away, staring at the creations in the chambers.

"Why would you continue a work you did not believe in?" The professor asked.

"This planet needs new life on it. If for nothing else, to balance with my people. Every species needs a predator." Inak answered.

"…And you are the predator?" Nick interjected.

"You seem to want that to be true. It is not, we may very well have been the prey. Never discredit yourselves as humans, and your ability to destroy those around you. I saw the other time lines and universes through my omni-viewer. On another planet, humans waged nuclear war. On another, they destroyed their planet by destroying their moon. I watched as one race abused their environment and the planet ripped itself apart. Humans are more deadly than any alien race you might encounter." Inak flew into a rage as his words continued. "I saw one race called the Ancients, or as they like to call themselves, the Egyptians. They enslaved so many of my people. Killing them at will, if they wished. They made a game of it. They came through the gateway and took them by force. Lifeforces mean nothing to them, as long as the Ancients are pleased."

"What is an omni-viewer, and how do you see the worlds?" The professor asked.

"Come with me, I will show you." Inak led them to a back chamber which appeared to be his living space. "Watch and learn."

As he picked up several of the crystals and placed them in front of a round opening in the wall, it began to light up, and a swirl of colors wove together to show an image. In the viewer, another earth was shown. One where life had been destroyed by war. There was little left on the planet, and no life to be seen. Inak than changed the configuration of the crystals and showed another planet devoid of life and covered in ice.

"You see, humans did this, and if I keep changing the viewer, you will continue to see the destruction your kind brought upon the worlds you inhabited."

"That does not mean all worlds turned out that way. Our Earth was different. We survived and grew." Nick insisted.

"And waged war with other colors and religions. You pushed your planet to the verge of destruction. When you left, your planet was dying of global warming." Inak said as he moved the crystals and their planet showed before them.

"How did you know which was our Earth?" The professor asked.

"I tracked you from the moment you arrived here. Your movements set off my alert system and I scanned you. Do not forget, I am from a very advanced time."

"Can you show us how to get home?" Nick asked.

"Yes, I could, but it would cost you a payment. I believe that is what you call it."

"What do you want?" The professor asked.

"Nothing much…just your DNA. With it, I can finish the experiments, and bring life to the children created here. This planet would have a chance of growing."

"Not a chance in hell." Shabakaa grumbled.

"He's right, we cannot allow you to play god to these creations." The professor insisted.

"Very well, but it would not be the first time we created life on a planet. We already did it on the planet Mars long ago. Their waring ways led to their destruction. If you do not wish to cooperate, then leave and face the land outside the protective halls. You may not find it so easy to survive. It is your choice, but make it soon. My time here will end whether I finish this work or not. Enjoy the Savage Land as I call it." Inak returned to his work as the group looked to each other.

Chapter Seven: The Savage Land

As they turned to leave, Nick looked back once more at Inak. He trailed behind as the group entered the hall. Before them stood a group of reptile figures resembling Inak in appearance, but more barbaric and unintelligent.   The creatures surrounded the group as Nick called to Inak for help.

As he appeared in the doorway, Inak raised his hand to the others, and flashed a bright red light at them from a crystal. The primitive creatures drew back in fear, as he ordered them to leave. They bobbed back and forth like wild animals being taken away from a kill.

"You may safely leave now. Be warned, the Jabberwock can easily be scared, but they will be back. Next time, in greater numbers than before. If I were you, I would go quickly. I will not always be around to protect you." Inak said as he turned to leave.

They moved away quickly, but as they walked deep from within the side hallways, they heard the hissing sound of the Jabberwock. They were hiding in the shadows waiting…watching their every move. Staying in the halls, would mean capture and probably death.

"We need to get out of here quickly." Nick said as he started to run, his voice vibrating from the movement.

"I agree." The Professor replied.

"Yeah, but what about our friend the dinosaur just outside the opening?" Shabakaa spoke with a scared tone.

"There was one dinosaur, and an army of Jabberwock, you decide which we can avoid the best." Nick called out.

As they ran for the opening, they saw nothing to stop them from leaving. Behind them, the Jabberwock had amassed a group, and were coming up from behind. As the travelers flew out into the sunlight, they looked around, they were alone. Behind them, the army reached the opening and stopped dead in their tracks. The Jabberwocks in the front threw their hands up to block the light which shown through the doorway.

Nick watched them and their movement. Every time they attempted to come forward and run for the group, the Jabberwock drew back from the sunlight. He was sure of it now; they could not see in the light. They were nocturnal creatures. It made sense why they lived in the darkened halls.

"Professor, stop!" Nick shouted. "We're safe for now. They cannot come into the light. It blinds them."

"Yes, I believe you are right. For now, we are OK, but when nightfall comes…that might be another matter."

"We have to find shelter. Some place they cannot get into, and we can exist until morning." Nick said as he looked around and saw nothing.

They walked for hours through the prehistoric land. Along the way, they encountered many creatures they would have seen in an Earth museum. They were reminded along the way, that many of these creatures, while spectacular, were also deadly. More than once, they ran for whatever shelter they could find.

"The temperature here is as bad as in Egypt." Emma said waving a scarf around her face to try to get some relief.

"Egypt was never this bad, it only felt that way because you came from a different climate." Shabakaa snapped back at her.

"I didn't mean to offend; I was just saying I am hot and thirsty. Not to mention hungry." Emma just realized they had no food or water.

"Yes, I realized that some time ago, but I was hoping to find some safe place to be before I brought it up." The professor responded with an uneasy sound in his voice.

"What about that?" Shabakaa said pointing behind the professor.

As the group turned, they all looked at the temple, that had been partially hidden from view by vines growing around the front of it. They walked cautiously towards it, being afraid from all they had encountered so far. They knew anything could be inside. That scared them more than the land they walked through.

"So, who is brave enough to go scouting?" Emma said nervously laughing.

"I'll go." Nick knew it had to be done quickly, being that night was coming.

Nick tried to move the door that covered the opening to the temple. Nothing could shift it. As he became frustrated, he leaned against the outer wall and felt the shape of a stone press into his back. There again, was a shape like the crystal. If he inserted it, the door would open, or so he hoped. As he placed the bottom of the crystal into place, the door slowly slid between a hollow part of the stone wall.

As the door pulled away, a strange glow from within began to come from the doorway. The temple was lit by large groupings of crystals. Nick stepped inside, not knowing what to expect. To his amazement, the structure was empty of life. He walked around the room and studied the objects within. In one corner was a stone head, which looked very much like Inak. This was no regular temple; it was a Jabberwock place of remembrance.

Nick left quickly…if he could get in, then the Jabberwock could too.

Chapter Eight: Survival Quest

"We can't be here!" Nick screamed. "This place is a temple for the Jabberwock. There is a shrine inside to one of them."

"Calm down Nick. This place looks like it has not been entered in years." The professor tried to reassure him.

"It is lit inside. Someone has been here."

"Look Nick, it is lit by crystals. Maybe they were activated, when you opened the door. It doesn't mean anyone has been here recently. The door was even covered by vines. If you had not pushed them to the side, you would have never gotten inside." The professor was determined to win this argument.

"I agree with the professor. This place has not been used for some time. Maybe we can block the door somehow or stand guard." Emma was tired and really did not want to debate the issue any further.

"Ok, I give. We have found structure, for however long we have to be here. Now we need food and water." Nick said looking around.

"Those look like fruit." Shabakaa said as he pointed to the alien looking trees growing just over the hill.

They closed the temple, and headed towards the group of trees. As they stared at the strange giant shapes, they were reminded of large melons. As few of the lower handing fruit were within reach, and they picked one.

The professor produced a knife from his pocket, and cut into the fruit, realizing it was just like a cantaloupe inside. Grabbing several, they headed back to the temple, just as a dinosaur came up behind the trees and started to eat. Shabakaa looked back in fear, as he heard the chewing sounds coming from behind them.

"I think we are OK, that one just wants a fruit salad." Nick said laughing. "Now, we can drop these off, and figure out how to get water."

After retrieving two bowls from the temple, the group divided and went in opposite directions. They had only a couple of hours of light left. They realized the danger of being out in the dark. It was a risk they had to avoid.

Time was running out as Nick and Emma walked down through a ravine in the rocky area. It was there, Nick heard a familiar sound. It started out low and as he got closer, it grew. It was a water fall splashing down the rock formation.

Grabbing hold of Emma's hand, he pulled her to the side as he watched to see who or what might be there as well. Looking around, he saw a couple of small animals, but not ones that posed a threat. Moving quickly, he and Emma made their way to the edge of the falls, just feet from where they had been hidden.

"How do we know if it is safe for us to drink?" Emma said as she stared into the clear water.

"We don't, that is why one of us has to be a guinea pig.   I guess I am it." Nick said bringing the bowl up to his mouth.

"Wow, you are a chauvinist aren't you." She insisted.

"What do you mean?"

"I can be a guinea pig, what does it always have to be the guy who goes first." Emma blasted him as she folded her arms.

"OK, I will tell you why I want to go first." Nick responded. "Because this stuff could kill me. It could be poison. I would rather not have you die to find out."

Emma unfolded her arms, and she realized what he was about to do. Her expression changed as she reached out for Nick. Before she could comfort him or argue anymore, he took a big gulp of the water.

He closed his eyes, and made a face, as if he was waiting for something to happen. Nothing did. He slowly opened his eyes and looked into hers. The water appeared to be good. He was hopeful it would be, being so many animals were drinking and all of them looked healthy.

"I think we are going to be alright." He said taking another drink.

He and Emma drank, and then refilled the bowl as they headed back to the temple. The night had begun to fall all around the Savage Land as the light of day faded. They rushed back trying not to spill their water.

Moments before reaching the temple, they heard the familiar hiss of the Jabberwock. They had wasted no time in going out that evening, to scout for their human prey. Nick pulled Emma back off the trail they followed as the watched several of the creatures walking in the direction if the Temple.

"I knew they used the place. I told you so." Nick whispered.

"No, look, they are going past. They are just searching for us. I hope the professor and Shabakaa have managed to stay safe."

"I wouldn't bet on it. Look, there they are, and the Jabberwock are headed right for them." Nick handed the bowl of water to Emma and prepared to run.

Nick flew from his hiding place and ran to help his friends. As he remembered the small flashlight he kept in his back pocket. If the creatures were blinded by light, he had an idea what to do.

The Jabberwock threw their nets over the professor and Shabakaa and prepared to tie them, as Nick came up from behind. He aimed his light into their eyes, and they threw their arms up as they were blinded. He reached for the nets and pulled at them allowing the two to go free. Aiming his light, he continued to blind the Jabberwock as they all escaped.

Arriving back at the temple, Nick pulled the crystal from his pocket, and they all quickly moved inside. Emma sat the water down on a pedestal and joined the others in searching for a way to block the door. In a corner, Nick found a large wooden beam that would fit behind the door, and not allow it to slide back into its track. For the moment they felt safe.

Outside the Jabberwock gathered in numbers. They surrounded the temple and beat on the door with stones and anything else they could find. They were determined to claim their prey.

Chapter Nine: Escape from Earth Prime

Emma sat in the corner listening to the pounding on the door. With every loud noise, she rocked back and forth. The Jabberwock were in her head. The others tried to ignore the sounds. They knew it was safe in the temple, there was no other way in, that they knew of.

The professor gathered their pile of fruit and cut into it. They had to eat to keep their strength up. There was no telling when their next meal would come. Inside the temple, were flat discs that looked like plates. The professor took four of them and placed the fruit for each of them to eat.

As he passed them around, Nick took a plate over to Emma, who was still rocking and staring at the door. He reached it out to her, but she did not take it. Her eyes were locked onto the door and she was not letting go of it.

"Emma, can you hear me." Nick spoke softly. "You have to eat. You'll need your energy."

Energy for what? If they get through the door, we will all be dead." She could barely get the words out.

"No, it won't happen that way. We have the door jammed. They can't break through. This place is indestructible. They cannot get in, and besides, they can only keep this up until morning. When the sun comes up, they will be gone." Nick tried his best to comfort her. "Now, please eat this."

"I was such a horrible person to you in the past. I need to apologize." She searched for the words, but did not know how to say it all to him.

"It's Ok, it's in the past. We have a whole future ahead of us. Now eat." He insisted.

"Nick, what do you make of this?" The professor asked.

"It is similar to the dialing table. Well, except the crystals are in a different layout. I wonder what it does." Nick leaned down and studied the crystals. "It is missing one crystal just like the one I have. Maybe we should try it."

"Nick, we don't know what that is. It isn't a travel device. There is no doorway. This could be dangerous." Shabakaa said pulling Nick's arm back.

"I understand your concern, but if we do not try this, we will never know." Nick pulled his arm free and raised the crystal in front of him.

He hesitantly moved the crystal over the table and just above the place it should have been. Breathing deeply, he paused and sat the crystal into place. Then for a moment, nothing. He turned to look at the professor, as a bright red glow began to emit from the stone head of the Jabberwock in front of the table.

"Greetings to you, the survivors of the great cataclysm. I am Dracon. I was once a leader in the great race of Jabberwock. Before the nuclear war claimed the majority of our people and wiped this planet of all advanced technology. We were once a peaceful race, but the arrival of a war like race from space, doomed us all. I am leaving this record for any who survived. This planet is doomed. Leave here if the technology still exists. Use the gate system and save yourself. There are many planets and times to pick from. Save yourselves while there is still time. Included in the archives, are instructions for gate usage, May peace follow you." Then the voice faded.

Nick studied the table and saw that there were discs placed in storage underneath. He pulled out the first, but the writing was like pictographs and he did not understand. Then he looked at the remaining stack. They all agreed, that since they would be stuck in there until morning, to go through all of them and learn all that they could.

On the table was a set of prongs that were spaced apart just enough to hold a disc. Nick placed the first inside, and the holder began to turn until it was spinning at a fast speed, the disc disappeared and a light ring formed in its place. In that ring another Jabberwock appeared.

The first disc told of their great civilization called Earth Prime and showed images of how far they had advanced in science and technology. Their civilization had just achieved space flight before the cataclysm. It was believed that when they achieved space flight, an alien race took notice of them and realized their advancement.

The second disc told of the war with the Replicants. They were a dominant race of creatures, that traveled through solar systems seeking new and advanced technology to add to their own. They operated as one singular being, as part of a hive. All working as one to make the best decisions and calculated moves to conquer and absorb other people, their technology and wipe the original civilization out of the galaxy.

"Nick, this does not seem right. Inak said he came from his future, to help his people. He couldn't have, these people had no future. Could he have come from their past, and does not realize he traveled to the wrong time?" Emma said as she studied the images flashed before them.

"Maybe, that does make sense, but how could he not know?" Nick shook his head as he loaded the next disc. As the disc spun, it flashed light and glowed but no information came to the display. Nick changed disc after disc, they were all the same way. Then he tried the last one and it displayed the obelisk and the images of gate travel.

They watched and waited for the information they needed, but as the disc played, it started to garble. Just as the information on the crystal usage started to show, the disc stopped spinning. Something had damaged it and the others in the stack. Their only hope of learning how to use the gate, had disintegrated right in front of their eyes.

Chapter Ten: Inak's Escape to the Past

As the light of the sun washed over the war-torn planet, the Jabberwocks retreated deep within their dark shadowed halls. They found their rest chambers, and for the next twelve hours would sleep and regenerate. As they disappeared, the dinosaurs once again awakened and prepared to feast.

Nick and Shabakaa pulled free the wooden bean, which had wedged the door throughout the night. With it gone, the door slowly started to slide backwards into the wall, allowing sunlight to fill the opening where it had once been.

Stepping out, Emma covered her eyes, and searched the landscape for safety. She sighed as she realized they Jabberwock really were gone.

Gathering the group together, they sat out towards the old ruins, they needed to see Inak.

Quickly they made their way to the large stone courtyard. Looking up Nick saw the painting on the wall again. "Beware the Jabberwock." Now it made sense to him. These creatures were savage. Perhaps the land outside had been misnamed. The Jabberwock home should have been the Savage Land.

As they entered the familiar darkened hall, Nick staired at the wall once again. As he moved slowly, he saw the reference to Earth Prime. They were on Earth after all, just in another dimension and time. His mind spun in all directions as he tried to understand, if the planet he was on was Earth Prime, then which earth did he come from.

Deep in the hall, the light started to disappear, leaving them vulnerable to any Jabberwock who may not have been sleeping. Nick studied the hall as they walked. In one corner, on the floor, were torches that had once been used and discarded.

Nick grabbed them and handed one to Shabakaa. "Got a light?" Nick asked him.

"Why would you assume I smoke?" Shabakaa responded.

"I'm sorry, I did not mean to insult you."

"It's Ok. Yes, I do have one, I just don't know why you assumed."

They lit the torches and the glow from their fires filled the corners of the hall. This time they could see where they were going. They made their way through until they found Inak's door. Nick raised the crystal and activated the opening.

"Inak, are you here?" Nick called out as they entered and closed the door behind them. They were not ready for another run-in with the Jabberwock so soon.

"Nick, did you realize there was an absence of Jabberwock in the halls?" The professor asked.

"Yeah, I did. What do you think that is all about?" He answered.

"It is simple, they are in regeneration. All creatures need sleep. Especially if you are an uncivilized hunter race." Inak spoke from the rear of the room. "Why have you returned? I thought our association was over."

"Last night we took refuge in a temple. There, we found historical records of this planet. Inak, I don't think this is your past. I think when you time-traveled, you came to your future." Nick tried to explain.

"You can save your words. I know of what you speak. I have suspected it for some time now. Too many events since I arrived led me to the same conclusion. My people were doomed. If they had only not explored space on that day in history, the

Replicants would probably have not found this planet."

"…And they would not have set the whole event in process." Emma finished his thought.

"Yes, young human. You are right. I have considered the situation. This whole event could have been avoided. Perhaps, it still could be. With one simple action on my part, I could save my people."

What do you mean?" The professor asked.

"It is simple, I will time-travel back to my time and attempt to change the course of this planet. If I can convince my leaders to stop the launch into space, we may very well change this time-line."

"Wait, if you do that, what will happen to us? We are stuck here." Emma asked.

"You will have to leave before I travel." Inak said, looking at them with his huge oval shaped eyes.

"We don't know how to leave here." Emma screamed as she became frustrated with him.

"You came through the gate; you shall leave the same way. I will guide you to a functioning gate doorway. If we leave soon, we should have no opposition from the Jabberwock."

As they turned to open the door to leave, a hunting party from the Jabberwock waited just outside. Nick reached for the counter beside him, where he found a weapon. Holding it in front of himself, he screamed at the Jabberwock.

"You are wasting your words. They are primitive, barbaric if you wish. They do not have the ability to speak or understand your words. Save your energy for the fight to escape here." Inak said as he walked forward and raised a triangular crystal in his claw-like hand.

As Inak aimed the crystal, he told the others to close their eyes. As they did, he turned loose the power of the crystal which filled the entire chamber and hall with a blinding light which took the sight from the Jabberwock. The creatures fell to the ground in a totally disoriented state.

"They will not bother us any longer." Inak said in a grumble as he looked down on his people lying about him on the stone floor.

"What did you do?" Nick asked.

"I blinded them."

"For how long?" Nick knew there was more to what Inak had said.

"They are blinded forever. That is why I asked you to close your eyes. If not, you would have been blinded too."

Nick drew back, offended by how easily the creature would betray his own race. He was now scared that Inak would flee back to his own time and leave them there to be destroyed when the timeline was reset. Still, he had to follow this alien creature if he wanted to survive.

Chapter Eleven: Betrayed by the Jabberwock

They wondered through the corridors, passing through many different tunnels and hidden places, before arriving at transport center. Nick looked on in awe of the once great hub. There were many different gateway openings, and chambers for traveling to different times. In front of the chambers was a type of subway, that led deeper underground to places unknown to them.

Nick watched as Inak swayed back and forth, while he walked towards the time-travel chambers. He doubted their would-be savior and could not contain it any longer. Grabbing the professor's arm, he pulled him to the side.

"Do you feel something is wrong?" Nick asked.

"Yes, I have had that feeling since we arrived at his door. He wants to go back to his own time. What does he care if we can leave here? We could just be collateral damage. As long as he can leave, he thinks he can save his people."

The professor's words were grim but true. They had to gain control of the situation that was unfolding. Inak still held the crystal in his hand. He could use it against them, and Nick knew it. He had to get the crystal away from him.

As they approached the chambers, Inak looked in their direction. Then he turned to the others. "I promised you a way home, it is here in front of you." He said as he turned and pointed towards the gateways. "You only have to enter the coordinates of the planet and time you wish to travel to."

"That is the problem. We do not know how to return home. We left our world accidentally. No one taught us how to do this." Nick was becoming frustrated.

"If I do not know where to send you to, then I cannot find your home world. I need a point in time and space where your world should be. That is how the crystals work. They can only open a gate to an intended place or one which has already been programmed. When you came here, someone had already used your gate. I cannot help. I have no knowledge to make this happen." Inak said as he turned and walked towards the time-travel chamber.

"What do we do now? We cannot stay here." Shabakaa said kicking a stone that lay on the floor.

"We have other problems." Nick said as he pointed to the Jabberwock hunter group that was forming in the hall they had just left.

"I have had just about enough of this." Emma screamed. "I want out of here, and I don't care where, as long as they are gone."

As she finished speaking, the creatures began to head their way. As Nick turned to Inak, he watched as he climbed into his chamber. Nick ran to him, furious that the creature was betraying them. Nick arrived just as the lid was slowly closing.

"How could you do this to us?" Nick screamed.

"I have sympathy for your situation, but if I do this my people might have a chance." Inak raised his voice.

"They are going to kill us. Is there nothing you can do?" Nick pleaded.

Reaching his hand out of the chamber, Inak gave Nick the crystal he had carried with him. "Aim it at them, and the crystal will do the rest."

"Thank-you, but what about the gateway?"

"Use an address that is already in the system. It will at least get you to a safer place. Or not." Inak said as the lid closed completely and the inside filled with light. In no time his body was gone from sight.

Nick made his way back to the others. He motioned for them to move behind him. He did not need words; they knew what was about to happen. Lifting the crystal in front of him, he mentally focused on the enemy and closed his eyes.

The light flew forward like before, but this time in a more intense way. The red beam blasted its way through the entire group of Jabberwock disintegrating their bodies as they fell to the ground. By the time Nick stopped, there were only mounds of dust, where the creatures once stood.

Nick looked on in disbelief at what he had done. He had never killed anything in his life. He told himself it was for survival. In the animal kingdom, animals killed for survival of the fittest. Still in his mind, he had killed living things.

"We had better get out of here before Inak changes the time-line. I didn't fight through this just to cease to exist." Nick said as he motioned them to move towards the gateways.

"How do we choose one?" Emma asked.

"I have no idea, nothing about using this makes sense unless, you have an address to go to. What if you go someplace worse?"

"Then we gate the hell back out of there until we find a better place or hopefully go home." The professor answered.

The gateways were slightly different from what they had seen before. When they left Egypt, the gate was very simple and scaled down. The ones before them were more modern and futuristic.

Nick put his hand on the first one he walked up to and it lit up. A simple word was echoed from its audio… "Destination." Nick thought about it for a second and then a smile came across his face. He wanted to go to Egypt. Could it be that simple?

Nick turned to the others. "What if it knows where Egypt is?" He said with excitement. "Maybe it will fill the address in for us."

"It's worth a try." Shabakaa added. "Just get us out of here."

Nick turned back to the gate and placed his hand onto it again. As it did before, once more it asked for his destination. Nick cleared his throat and said "Egypt". The machine acknowledged him and returned with… "Searching".

After several minutes, the machine spoke again. "Destination acquired," echoed from the machine as Emma became excited and hugged Nick. "Please move forward to the gate for departure."

As the gate began to glow a bright blue, the machine notified them it was ready for entry. The group walked forward, hopeful they were going home. They were all still a little hesitant that the destination they were going to, could be more deadly than the one they were leaving.

As the gate began to close in around them, looking back, Nick saw the area that they were in before changing. Inak had made his way home and changed his history. They could not be leaving at a better time. A minute later and they would have been erased from the planet's timeline.

Chapter Twelve: The Curse of Cleopatra

As the gate surrounded their bodies, the four travelers were ripped through space and time, into another dimension. As they passed through the gate, many worlds were opened up to them. Each dimension they passed, was a part of the multiverse. Many similar places existed with slight changes, where some places are totally changed.

This time, traveling through the gate was different, they could see where they were going. The feeling of illness was not there. As they approached the end of the wormhole, a spinning wave of blue light appeared before them. Stepping out, was a more pleasant experience.

As they walked down off the platform, that held the obelisk, they looked around. The environment was hot, and the place covered with sand. It could have been Egypt, and possibly their Earth. There were no landmarks to identify such as ancient ruins.

Nick turned to the professor. "Well, are we home?"

"I have to say, I have no idea where we are. I am just happy to be free of the Jabberwock. Oh, and to be off the night's menu." The professor said laughing.

"At least, Inak gave us a way out. And in doing so, still got his wish." Emma added.

"Something about that scares me." Shabakaa spoke up. "The Replicants existed in his universe. Can they still exist in ours, or somewhere we end up?"

"I guess so. It just depends on the timeline, and if one little thing happens to bring them into existence." The professor lowered his head, knowing they very well could show up anywhere they went. "For now, let's just worry about where we are, and how to find some shelter from the sun."

They decided to move to a higher elevation so they could see what lay before them. A large sand dune was in front of them to the north. It was the best option at the time.

Climbing up the dune was an adventure in itself, as soon as they could move up a little, sand would slide down around them, making the climb slow and uncomfortable. Nick pulled Emma along behind him, as the climbed. Reaching the top, Nick looked out in front of him in disbelief.

As Emma looked up when she reached the top, she saw it too. They had found Egypt, just not the one they were looking for. The group gathered around each other as they looked at the grand pyramids before them.

The scene was as if Egypt was new, with bright shining outer shells. There were people there surrounded by advanced technology. The top of the pyramids had flying ships floating over them and beneath, an electrical charge flowed between them.

Nick looked on in disbelief as he watched what he had studied his whole life, come alive as a science fiction movie. He looked down, as guards on mechanical floating bikes flew through the city. Realizing they were in the open, nick grabbed onto the others and forced them to the ground before they were seen.

"Now, what do we do professor?" Emma asked.

"I honestly have no idea. I don't know if we are in danger, or are they friendly. I guess we need to study them, before making a decision."

"Agreed, we can't make rash decisions and get ourselves captured." Nick said as he slid closer to the sand.

"We still have to find shelter." Emma insisted.

"Look, over on the outskirts of the city, there is a well and what looks like unused tents. We can go there." The professor replied.

The group made their way down the side of the sand dune, trying not to be seen. The people of the city seemed to be going about their own lives and not looking for things out of the ordinary.

Nick led the way as the group ran for the back of a tent which was the closest to them. From inside, they could escape the sun, while seeing what the people were like. No one seemed to come in the direction of the small tent. They would be safe for a while.

While watching to make sure no one came towards them, Nick grabbed a bowl and headed for the well just feet from their hideout. The water was welcome, after going from one hot environment to the next. As Nick drank, he stared in amazement at the ships hovering just in front of him. He had always wondered if the pyramids on his earth had some strange function. He was sure the great pyramid of his Earth was a power station. Now he thought, perhaps he was right.

As Nick stared out into the sun, he saw a guard on one of the bikes heading towards them. He pulled back inside, in fear. How could they have been seen. He told the others as they prepared to hide any way they could.

Just outside the doorway to the tent, the bike stopped. The extremely muscled enforcer stepped off the floating bike and looked around. He did not come to the tent, but did pace back and forth through the area. Walking over, he took water from the well and poured it over himself. He seemed refreshed and not concerned with looking for anyone.

Nick stayed his ground, and tried to keep his eyes on the guard. They had come too far to be captured or enslaved. He was not going to allow it. He reached down to his pocket, and produced the crystal that Inak had given to him. He was prepared to use it if he had to. And then he thought about it. He had never been a violent person before, and now he was willing to take the life of an innocent man, just to ensure their freedom.

Just then, Nick dropped the crystal and it made a noise the guard could hear. The man moved in their direction to investigate. Nick grabbed the crystal and moved back as he cradled it and prepared to blast.

Mullins

Chapter Thirteen: The Gods of Egypt

As the guard moved closer to the tent, Emma felt her hands begin to shake. Her heart beat in her chest so loudly, she could feel it throughout her body. She was scared, not that the whole experience gating did not make her nervous anyway. The Jabberwock hunters pushed her to a limit shad not been to in many years.

She covered her mouth to stop the noises she knew she would make. Deep inside all she wanted to do was scream. She watched Nick, as he held tight to the crystal. She thought of him and his conflict. He did not want to kill anyone, reptile or human. That was, if this man approaching was human. She saw

Nick's hand shaking, it was more than she could stand.

Slowly, and quietly, she crawled up behind Nick and ran her hand down his back. She wanted him to know he had her support. Not that it would mean much if they were about to be captured. Nick leaned back into her for a moment. As their two bodies met, they both knew things had changed.

The guard moved closer to the tent doorway, as he scanned the grounds. He saw nothing and was confused, he thought that maybe he had imagined the whole thing. Just as he was about to enter the tent, another guard came from behind.

"The Queen has summoned us. We have to go." The second guard called to him.

"Ok, I just have to check to see what is in here."

"No, now. You know how the Queen is when someone is late. We have to go."

The first guard acknowledged him and turned his back to the tent. As he walked away, Emma released the air from her lungs, which she had dared not breathe deeply for fear of being heard. As he walked further away, she let out a little giggle. It was as if she was a child and had gotten away with something.

"The Queen has summoned them? This Egypt has a Queen." The professor had his curiosity peaked.

"Yes, but who is the Queen? Are we on the planet that the other Nick told us about?" Shabakaa spoke out.

"I don't know, like Inak said there are so many worlds in the multiverse and this could just be a variation." Nick said as he looked into Emma's eyes. "Nothing will happen to you. I swear it."

Nick's words fell on deaf ears, as Emma slumped down and staired at the sand beneath her. She knew, if in another reality she had been killed, then there was a chance it could happen again. The thought was paralyzing.

"We have to find a way to get inside the city and see who this Queen is and what this place is all about." The professor spoke as his mind began to race over the possibilities.

"Someone has to go inside. Someone who could pass for Egyptian." Nick said smiling at Shabakaa.

"No way. I won't do it. I didn't even want to come here in the first place." He defended himself. "Besides, you are only doing this because I was born in Egypt."

"Exactly, you can pass for one of them." Nick responded.

"Not if I do not go. I refuse."

"You can't refuse, we are all trapped here."
Emma grumbled at him.

Shabakaa grunted and drove his fist into the
sand. "Ok, I have no choice, but it does not mean I
have to like this. Oh, and I am not going alone."

"How will one of us be able to go with you?
We are very light skinned, we would stand out in the
crowd, if you know what I mean." Nick tried to
make him understand.

"Ah, but Nick, you have a tan and in the right
clothing, we could make you pass. Speaking of
which. What am I to wear? My clothing does not
scream other world Egypt."

Shabakaa had a point. As they looked around
the tent, they saw multiple storage boxes in the back.
A couple of them had clothing inside. Searching

through the many pieces, they found items appropriate for both of them to wear.

As they began to dress, Emma stood watching. Shabakaa looked up as he had begun to unbutton his pants. He cocked his head to the side and made a face that told her to look away. She did not take the hint.

"Look, I have to dress to go to the city and pretend to be one of them. I do not have to be an exhibitionist. So, with all due respect, turn away. The goods are not on show. My people do have some modesty you know."

Emma turned her back and did not look in his direction. They dressed quickly and prepared to leave. Nick looked down at his outfit. He was not convinced it was a good idea.

"What am I supposed to be, some kind of monk?"

"Precisely!" Shabakaa said laughing at him. "You might just learn to appreciate that outfit when we go out into the sun. It will protect you from the heat."

"I guess you are right. I just feel kind of weird wearing this."

As they prepared to leave, Emma walked up to Nick. "Come back to me."

"I'm not going anywhere. I promise." He said looking into her eyes.

She smiled at him, as he turned to leave. Stepping outside, the two walked across the hot sand covered ground to the city's entrance. As the drew closer, the met with many others on their way to the Queen. No one questioned their presence. They had accomplished their goal.

The center of the city was flooded with citizens who were summoned. The Queen's people were obedient, or at least it seemed. Nick and Shabakaa made their way through the crowd and tried to get as far forward as possible.

As they approached the platform where the Queen's throne was prepared, they had a perfect view for her entrance. They looked at each other and smiled. They were going to pull this off.

Music began to play, as the sounds of the crowd died down. A whisper went across the people, "She is coming." Nick looked up, as the Queen began to make her way forward. The people fell to their knees, but Nick did not. Shabakaa reached out and grabbed him, dragging him to ground, before the was noticed.

As Nick regained his balance, he glanced up to see her moving to the throne. His heart began to beat in his chest. The breathing quickened as he turned to Shabakaa and spoke. "Cleopatra."

Chapter Fourteen: Thoth the Great and Powerful

Nick held his breath as he listened to Cleopatra speak. His heart raced as his mind search for any way to escape the crowd and return to the others. Shabakaa glanced in his direction, it was obvious, Nick was heading for a breakdown. Still, they had no choice, they had to stay until it was over.

Nearly 30 minutes later, they were told to leave. Nick turned to Shabakaa and leaned in to him. "We have to get out of here. This is not going to end well." They agreed, and proceeded to leave, as a guard came up near them. They walked quickly and tried to go in a different direction, but he followed closely behind.

As they moved down a side street, there were many buildings and multiple doorways. Nick knew they had to choose one or they would be caught. As they rounded a corner, Nick grabbed on to Shabakaa and pulled him into an opening.

As they disappeared into the doorway, the guard passed. Nick doubled over, trying as hard as he could to catch his breath. Shabakaa leaned into the doorway, feeling a sense of relief that he had not been captured. They both laughed, before looking into the space they had hidden.

"Close the door. If you have business here, make it quick. My time is valuable." The voice called out.

"Hello, we are sorry to disturb you. We did not mean to interrupt." Nick called back, as he started to walk into the room where a glowing green light was seeping out.

"You have both disturbed and interrupted. Why do you people not understand how important my work is. I am the greatest mind in the history of man. One would think that would award me some amount of respect."

The figure of a man turned to them. It was he who lit the room, with his glow. Nick looked him up and down, and then through. He was a computer-generated hologram. Nick had seen them before, but something was different with this one. He was interactive.

"Are you Thoth, the most intelligent mind of Egypt?" Nick asked.

"I would be, and who are you two?" He asked.

"We are travelers. We are not from this place." Nick replied.

"That much, I am sure of. You came through the gateway, didn't you?"

"How did you know that?" Shabakaa asked.

"I am Thoth, I know everything. I also scanned your DNA. You are from another world in the multiverse. I would say the bigger question would be, why are you here?"

"We were pulled into the gateway, not knowing what it was. Now, we are lost, without a way home." Nick chose his words carefully; he was not sure of the extent Thoth would help them.

"I see your dilemma. So, you came to me to sort your problem." Thoth laughed, "Of course you did. If I have the time, I might help you. For now, I am much too busy to cater to your issues. You may come back to me in precisely one week. Same day, same time, I will grant you an audience."

"May I ask you a question?" Shabakaa spoke up.

"Oh look, it can speak. If you must."

"If I must what?"

"Ask me a question. Do it soon, I have much to do." Thoth became agitated.

"Are you a hologram or something else?"

"I am a man, whose intelligence has been transferred to a computer. My body which was not capable of holding all my abilities and intelligence failed. Before my death, I constructed this computer and means of existence. I am now greater than I have ever been. I will go on forever, as the most intelligent man in history, and be the god of the moon, wisdom, writing, hieroglyphs, science, magic, art, and judgment. Now, have I settled all your questions and interruptions?"

"Yes, I do believe so." Nick answered.

"Good, now be gone."

As Nick and Shabakaa turned to leave, they looked back as Thoth went about his work almost unaware if they had left or not. As they watched him turn, his hologram split into multiple versions of himself. Each of the holograms went to work on a different project, all at the same time, all in unison.

"I guess in immortality, he has attained the highest level of intelligence." Nick whispered.

"Thank-you, yes I have." The Thoth figures answered.

Nick and Shabakaa left the doorway and looked out into the bright sunlight as they tried to gain their bearings and return to the others. Perhaps they had found a way home after all.

Chapter Fifteen: New Egypt Earth 221

Nick studied the streets as they made their way towards the outskirts. As they walked, he staired up at the statues and golden walls filled with hieroglyphs. He had studied it all before, on his Earth, but there he was used to it all being in ruin or damaged by time.

When he turned to the right, and looked down the crowded path, he saw the Sphinx of that planet. A smile crossed his face as he stared at the head, and realized the face his own should have had all along. He was awestruck by the beauty of the construction.

"Shabakaa, you have to see this." Nick said as he grabbed his head and spun it in the right direction.

Shabakaa looked up at the wonder of it. "It is beautiful. It has not been destroyed by man or the elements. I could have never imagined this."

"It is amazing, is it not?" A voice came from behind them.

"Yes, it is." Nick answered.

"You must be new here." The woman spoke.

"Yes, we have only just arrived. The whole city is more than I could have ever imagined." Nick replied.

"My name is Iraya. Where did you come from?" She asked.

"A long way from here. You have probably never heard of it." Shabakaa answered.

"Does it have a name?" She pushed.

"Is there a reason you are interrogating us?" Nick asked.

"No, but the gateway opened today. It has not done that in decades. I did not even think it worked anymore. Then you show up from a mysterious far away land. Except, there are no faraway lands here. The planet is barren except for New Egypt. Now speak or die." She said as she raised her hand into the air.

As Nick looked up, he saw the shiny golden cuff around her wrist that led in metal strips to her fingers. She opened her hand and the metal began to glow as her power built up inside. She swung her hand just as Shabakaa flew out of the way.

Nick had hoped to not draw any attention to themselves. That hope was just dashed. Iraya continued her assault, throwing high intensity light beams at them, as they clawed their way off the ground and tried to run.

As Nick jumped to his feet, Iraya was ready and blasted him in the back. He fell to the ground writing in pain. He knew the fight was over. He could not fight back, he was paralyzed.

Shabakaa was more fortunate in finding his feet, and escaping while Nick was being taken away. He made his way down the side street and headed for the tent unseen by others. His heart raced as he flew into the tent and collapsed on the floor.

"What happened?" Emma screamed as she jumped to his side.

"They got Nick. Some woman named Iraya blasted him with this light ray and they took him away. I couldn't help him."

"Professor, we have to save him. What do we do?" Emma asked.

"We need to find out where they took him. We just can't do it now. We have to wait until night fall. Maybe then we won't stand out so much."

"I'll go back. I fit in with them." Shabakaa insisted.

"No, you can't go alone." The professor tried to convince him.

"I have to go back for him. If I had been paying attention, this would not have happened."

"I am sure you did all you could. For now, we wait." The professor was holding to his word.

Back in the city, Nick blinked his eyes and tried to regain consciousness. His vision was out of focus but he could see large shapes at first. Then everything came into view. He tried to move but his body was restrained. He looked down to the large straps that encircled his body.

He jerked back and forth trying to free his arms. It was no use; he was strapped in tightly. He looked around to see if anyone was there, but saw no one. While struggling, he let out a loud grunt. The sound echoed through the chamber.

"Now, now, young one, mustn't make all that noise. It was her again, Nick new it.

"What do you want with me?" He called out.

"Just a little conversation…and some answers." Iraya prodded him.

"I don't know anything that would help you."

"Oh, I think you do. Soon you will tell me all I want to know. You see this machine above you can do so many things. It can make you tell the truth, or do my bidding. I can even use it to change you into a totally different person than you are now. I could even use it to end you permanently." Iraya laughed as the words came out. "It's your choice."

"Ok, I will cooperate." Nick conceded to her.

Iraya began her interrogation. She learned of his time after leaving his Earth. She even learned of his fellow travelers. He had no choice but to tell everything, the mind control would allow him to do little else.

When she was done, Iraya freed Nick. He raised his eyes, but looked distant. She had changed him, but allowed him to live. Walking around him in circles, she smiled. "You are actually very attractive. That is one of the few reasons I let you live.

She led Nick to a private chamber, where she pulled out new clothing for him to wear. He removed his old outfit and when he put on the new, he was transformed. He was no longer a shy quiet looking nerdy guy. He had become attractive and confident in his body. The pants she gave him, fit tightly to his legs. The top was tight and framed the muscles he had always hidden.

Iraya led Nick to the full-length mirror in the room. As she turned him to look into it, he began to smile. "See, you are so much more than you have allowed yourself to be. I see you as a warrior. Now you look the part."

Nick turned and looked at the bands on his arms and the muscles that they showed. He was not as weak as he had led himself to believe. His mind had been changed. Iraya had given him something he had always wanted, and that was enough to make the mind control work.

"Now my beautiful one, you need to make your transformation complete. Capture those that you came with. Bring them to me, so I may interrogate them."

"Will they survive?" Nick forced out his words as he felt the change taking place.

"You, I have use of. Them, I am not so sure. They serve no purpose to me alive. Perhaps you could convince me to save them."

Nick looked down at the floor, it was like he was watching his world from the outside. He could not control the new version of him that had been reprogrammed. Iraya had done her job well, he was powerless. He could only watch and wait for the time he could seize control again.

Chapter Sixteen: Betrayal from Within

As Nick moved at Iraya's command, a tear ran down the side of his cheek. He struggled to fight the control she had over him. It was a useless battle. The feeling was like nothing he had ever experienced.

"Don't fight so my love." Iraya whispered in his ear.

"What do you have planned for me?" Nick asked.

"It is simple. In the end, you shall play host to my god, Anubis. Your role in life will be one of the most important of the gods." She said lifting a mask from its enclosure.

"The God of the Dead." He whispered.

"I see you know your history well. It will be an honor for you to help revive Anubis. He has been lost for so many years now. Many of our other gods have returned. Our Queen Cleopatra has seen to that." She continued.

"If your queen has the ability to restore the gods, then why has Thoth been made into a computer?" Nick asked.

"Because that arrogant egomaniac felt he was too good to return to human form. He refused to be reborn. He said the human body could not contain his greatness, and he was better in hologram form. That way he could multitask." She stopped to laugh. "I try to avoid him at all costs."

Nick looked hard at the mask as she came closer to him. He studied it, and remembered the many images he had seen. The jackal head was very well represented in Egyptian history.

As Iraya lifted the mask in front of him, Nick could see the computer design within it. There were lines on the surface, that made the design of the head, which were like computer circuit boards. This was not a traditional Egyptian creation; it was a computer.

When Iraya tilted the mask upwards, the eyes began to glow a blue color. She smiled as she ran her fingers around the computer lines. She took pride in the design that honored her god.

"When you place that on my head, what will happen?" He asked.

"When Anubis died, his essence was preserved in this mask. When you wear it, he will emerge again. In your body, he will find a new life. Again, he will guide spirits to the afterlife. And you…" She trailed off.

"…And I?" He asked.

"You will be a host. The vessel of a god."

"So, I will die." He said swallowing hard.

"You will not die; you will no longer control the actions of your body. You will be a witness to his greatness." She began to smile as her words impressed even herself.

She raised the mask up to Nick, and a joy came over her face, as she began to place the covering over his head. As soon as the mask was above him, the jaw lowered from its black metal hood, making a clicking sound.

Sliding the mask into place, the jaw returned to its original position fitting perfectly to Nick's face. Iraya stepped back, overjoyed at the look she had provided for her god. Nick was transformed into a man no one would recognize. He truly looked like the god he was about to become.

Nick felt strange in the mask. He was always a bit claustrophobic, but this was more. As the mask rested on his head, he heard the buzzing of the mask's computer come online. As he tilted his head upward, the eyes of the mask turned a brilliant blue color, much like the glow of neon light.

Iraya saw the light and fell to her knees. She kneeled before him, awaiting her instructions. Nick watched, as he felt the mask take full control. He felt sick to his stomach for a second. Then he lost control.

"Arise Iraya!" He commanded.

"My God Anubis, is it really you." She asked.

"Yes, I am back. You have resurrected me, and provided me with a fine young body. I am pleased."

"I have done my best my lord." She spoke looking down at the floor.

As Anubis moved closer to her, he reached out and put his hand under her chin. Slowly, he raised her face to look at him. Her body trembled, partly from fear, and partly from the god who stood before her.

"You have no need to fear. You pleased me today. I will reward you for your loyalty."

Nick watched as Anubis walked around the chamber. This is New Egypt? I see Cleopatra has built it well. This is all so advanced from the time in which I lived. I will need a companion to assist my learning of this new way of life. I would assume you are up for the position?"

"Yes, my lord. I live to serve you." She answered him.

As Anubis turned to look at her, his blue eyes flickered. The computer within was struggling to keep control, as Nick fought back. He had regained full strength, as Anubis was taking control. Anubis let out a loud noise as Nick forced the computer to lose control.

Iraya looked at him in confusion. The mask was not supposed to fail. She approached Nick and tapped round discs on the side of the mask causing the chin to flip upwards. Nick glared at her as she removed the mask. He was waiting for his opportunity.

Iraya cradled the mask like it was a child. She cared for it, and tried to discover how to repair it. As she turned her head and started to take it to a bench to examine it for damage, Nick followed closely behind.

As she sat it down, Nick moved closer. He watched her and looked for anything that might give him an advantage. It was then he saw the large metal pipe on the side table. When Iraya turned her back, Nick grabbed it and made his attack.

Iraya fell to the floor unconscious and unaware of what had hit her. When Nick was sure she was out cold, he ran for the door. He knew how to get out this time. He had been studying the place since he was captured. When he had made his way to the center of the city, he flew back the way he and Shabakaa had come in.

Iraya reached her hand to her head. The moisture she had just felt, was not from the heat. Moving a finger upwards, she examined what she felt, it was red and flowing. She was bleeding. As her memory came back, she was aware what had happened. Nick was gone.

A guard came into the chamber to do a routine check. He rushed to her side. Helping her to the floor. He asked if she was hurt badly.

"I will mend in time. If anything is hurt, it is my pride." She grumbled. "The prisoner has escaped."

"I will search for him. He could not have gotten far." He responded.

"No, leave him. He will be back, sooner than he thinks."

"What do you mean?" The soldier asked.

"He has been reprogrammed. He will act out his role that I buried deep in his subconscious. …And when he does, we will have them all."

Chapter Seventeen: The Rise of Anubis

Nick ran as hard as he could. He would not let himself be captured again. He felt sick to his stomach from the feeling Anubis' control had over him. He had no desire to let that happen again.

As he rounded the corner near the tent, he stopped dead in his tracks. Flashes of memory ran through his head. There were so many images of death, destruction. Nick shook his head; he didn't usually think of things like this. As his mind raced, he remembered the programming. He clinched his fist as his memories ripped at him, "What did that bitch do to me?"

He continued to run until he reached the opening of the tent. As he threw open the flap,

Shabakaa flew forward and tackled him to the ground. He had a punch aimed at Nick's face, as Emma screamed.

"Nick, my friend, you are alive." Shabakaa grabbed him into a hug.

"I won't be for long, if you keep flattening me like that."

"I did not know it was you. Look at these clothes. You look like one of the gods. What is this all about?" He asked.

"Yes Nick, what is this all about?" The professor added.

"I was captured and taken into a chamber, where a woman…" Nick tried to speak, but his words were cut off before he could finish.

"Where a woman did what?" Emma demanded an explanation.

"I don't know, it is as if my memory is missing. I don't understand." Nick tried to explain.

"It's Ok son, you are back with us now." The professor said helping him to his feet.

"It's a good thing you arrived when you did. We were about to go out looking for you." Emma spoke still looking at him oddly.

"Then, I am glad I caught you. We need to go to see Thoth as a group." Nick insisted.

"Why do we need to do that. He said not to come back to the exact time he told us." Shabakaa was confused.

"I don't know, he just told me to come and get you and bring you back." Nick's head spun as he continued to talk.

Words were coming from his mouth, but he was no longer in control. He was beginning to feel disconnected. There was a window in front of him, and he was watching as his life was passing in front. Iraya's mind control was working. She had control of his actions, and she was not even there.

As Nick tried to convince the group to leave with him, Shabakaa pulled Emma to the side.

"Something is not right. Thoth said to come precisely when he asked. He does not play and does not want to be disturbed."

"So, you are saying Nick is lying?" She asked.

"No, I don't know what I am saying. Or, maybe I do. Something about this is not right. Maybe I am paranoid, but this feels like we are being led into a trap." Shabakaa turned to stare at Nick.

"How do we prove it is a trap?" Emma asked.

"I don't know. I guess go along with it until it gets dangerous?" He questioned his own logic.

"If he is lying or been brain washed, then let's find out how much?" Emma said, as she moved back to Nick's side.

Nick looked up at her as she approached. As she moved closer, she moved her hand to Nick's left cheek and pulled him into a kiss. Nick wrapped his arms around her and held tight. Emma knew then, the man in front of them was not Nick.

Shabakaa called out. "Get a room you two." He had to do something to save Emma.

Emma turned back to Shabakaa and pulled the professor along as she whispered, "That may look like Nick, but it's not him. We have never kissed since I have known him. Someone else is in control. It's a trap."

Nick finished looking out the doorway and turned to them. "We better leave now. The area is clear of guards."

"Sure Nick, we are ready when you are." The professor answered.

They all set off together in the direction of the city center. Nick led them through the streets and down side alleys, that he should have had no knowledge of. When they passed by the entrance to Thoth's private chamber, Nick guided them away. He told them; they were to meet in another location.

Shabakaa looked at the others and shook his head. Nick ushered them on, not stopping or paying attention to guards. Nick appeared to be on a mission, but no one knew who it was for.

Emma grabbed hold of Nick and stopped him in his tracks. She was determined to figure out what was going on. Nick looked at her innocently, as she stared into his eyes. He looked the same. There was no doubt he had not been switched, but mentally he seemed like another person.

"Stop Nick, or whoever you are! Enough already." She demanded. "Where the hell are you leading us?"

"To Thoth, we already talked about it." He answered.

"Save it, I am not buying it. Your game was up with the kiss. We have never been together. Hell, we couldn't even stand each other until this trip. Your little game is over."

"I know." Nick said as he staired deep into her eyes. "I was trying to let you know before it was too late. I figured you would get it. I imagined a false memory of us when she scanned me. I was hoping it would cause them to make a mistake and it did. Just too late I suppose. You see, they are coming for you now. Run!"

Chapter Eighteen: Children of the Gods

Nick stood still as the others ran in different directions. A smile crossed his face, as Iraya approached. She carried the mask of Anubis in her hands. Fully functional again, she was ready to bring back her god.

"Are you smiling because you attacked me and won? Or are you my obedient servant again."

"I am no servant; I am your god." Nick raised his voice as he took hold of the mask.

Holding the mask up over his head, he released the jaw, and put the covering over his face. The electrical circuits lit up and the eyes once again shined blue. He laughed as the power washed over him.

From a side street, Emma watched. She put her hand to her mouth. She wanted to scream but that would accomplish nothing. There was no other way she knew of that could save him. At the time, she did not even know how to save herself.

From behind her, Emma heard noises. As she turned, before her was a transparent man, whose glow emitted all around. She moved backwards and prepared to run when he reached out for her.

"Fear not. I mean you no harm. I was asked to help your group get home." He tried to calm her.

"You are Thoth. These people are trying to capture us. You are one of them. How could you mean us no harm?" She asked

"Yes, I am Egyptian. I did come with their group when they settled here. Let me assure you, I am not one of them. I simply exist alongside them. They bother me. They are less than important." He insisted.

"I don't understand, they are real, you are hologram. How can they still be alive after all this time?" Emma was confused.

"It is simple, they are not the original Gods of Egypt. Each one is a new host who has taken the role of the God, when the Ancient Ones died for whatever reason."

"How is that possible?"

"It is simple, each god has a particular item in their possession. With Cleopatra, it is a bracelet shaped like an asp. She liked the novelty of it since she supposedly died that way.   Hathor has a necklace, Horus has an amulet shaped like a falcon, Ra has the outline of a metal hawk rising from the sun attached to his face, the list goes on. Each item is a computer link that has passed their essence into a new human host. They are new incarnations of the gods. The people on this planet are the children of the gods."

"Then, why do you not have a body?" She asked.

"It would only slow me down. This way, I can split into as many versions of myself as I deem necessary. When I came to be a hologram, the technology that I used to recreate them, did not exist. I invented it, and gave them new life."

"Now, Nick has become one of them."

"Anubis to be exact. Though I did not intend for him to receive the mask. It was not my doing. I had it saved for a future visitor."

"There are all kinds of people walking around here. Why not use it on one of them?"

"Simple, they cannot be a host. Their molecular make-up excludes them. The hosts in the past have been ones who came through the gate, or were retrieved from visits to Earth."

"You just abducted people?"

"No, we gave them the opportunity to be gods."

"There are no words to tell you how disgusting that is. You took away their free will. They had lives, and people who loved them." Emma raged on.

"Yes and no. When I made the arrangements, I sent out emissaries that went back in time and retrieved people who were meant to die. Their lives were about to end. Their loved ones would have thought them dead anyway. This way, they were allowed to continue in life, just not the one they had." Thoth tried to make her understand.

"It is still wrong. Although I understand your reasoning." Emma leaned into the building beside her. "Can this be undone?"

"Yes, it the human has not been subjected to the computer's control for long. This process is not forced on anyone who would have had a life in any other way."

"No, you are wrong. Nick was forced into this. We came here because we were lost. We had no intentions of staying. We only wanted to learn how to return to our Earth." Emma defended herself and the group.

"Ah, I see. Iraya has been tampering again. She fancies herself a god. She is just one of the children. She had no business doing this without me. She will be dealt with, I promise you."

"I don't really care as long as we can get Nick back to his original self."

"Being he is wearing the mask now and voluntarily; we have little time left. Where are your friends?"

"I don't know, we all went in different directions."

"Then they were probably captured by the guards. Come with me."

Emma followed, as Thoth glided above the ground. She had to move quickly to keep up with him. As he flew forward, he made no sounds and spoke no words. He did look around from time to time, to observe the children of the gods. He rarely ever came out among them. To him, they were a waste of his time. It amused him, to float so effortlessly through them, observe, and feel so above them.

As they turned a corner, Emma saw the professor and Shabakaa in shackles being led away.

They were prisoners of the queen, trespassers in New Egypt, and slated for death.

Chapter Nineteen: Anubis Returns

Thoth threw a transparent arm in front of Emma. "Stop! Those are the queen's guards. This may be worse that I thought."

"You mean we cannot save them?" Emma spoke, sounding defeated.

"I have learned to allow the queen her room to rein."

"So, what the hell do we do." Emma became furious.

"Temper, temper, young one. We wait and watch. This is how we learn and then when the time is right, we move." Thoth said as he watched the prisoners being taken away.

Inside of Cleopatra's chamber, she watched as Nick moved before her. She studied him from head to toe. She smiled at the thought of another god returning. Their numbers would not only increase, but by one of the most powerful of the gods. With such power, she could lead the others to conquer other worlds. Turning to look away, she thought of the Earth. Her former home, would be one of the first she would enslave.

"Are you pleased my queen?" Iraya asked her.

"Very much so. He is magnificent. I couldn't have chosen better myself." Cleopatra said smiling as she took her throne. "We have been hindered too long by Thoth. If it were up to him, Anubis would still be locked away in that digital world we were placed in.

Nick listened to everything that was said. He was alert and aware. He could think for himself, but every time he tried to move or make his body move, Anubis seized control of his muscles. He was powerless to remove the helmet. With each attempt to fight back, he felt Anubis gaining power. The transformation was almost complete.

Arriving at the door, the guards announced that they had captured the prisoners. Cleopatra allowed them to enter, as she studied the travelers. She made a face, and look harder at the professor. Rising to her feet, she walked over to him.

"On your knees slave." She ordered.

When the professor failed to go down, a guard came from behind and kicked him in the back of his left knee. He fell to the floor in pain, as Cleopatra started to walk circles around the two of them. She knew she had seen him before, but where?

"I know you. I am good with faces, especially those of men. You…have been here before. …And you... There was another with you as well. A female, I remember it all now. She was rebellious." Cleopatra paced as she recalled the past incident. "I know her name…Emma. Something about you two though. You are the same, but also different."

Outside the doorway, Thoth and Emma arrived. From where they were standing, they could hear every word. Emma tried to watch without being seen. Thoth however, could see into the room being his sensors were all through the city. He watched in anticipation of what the queen was doing.

"You came through the gate, didn't you? Which means, you are from a different dimension. I thought you looked younger. Now, where is the girl. She should still be with you. Unless she met some horrible fate. I know the one who was here before, died horribly. Right there." She said pointing to a corner of the room. "She made the mistake of challenging me. Her mistake, it did not end well."

As Cleopatra laughed, Nick turned to face her. Even with Anubis in control, he still felt the rage of anger shoot through his body. As Anubis raised his head, a flash of blue light entered his eyes. Nick had gotten Anubis' attention.

Emma covered her mouth with her hand. Her fear was overtaking her. She had been terrified since she learned of how her counterpart had died. It was too much for her. Thoth turned and scanned her body as he became aware her heartbeat was racing.

"Calm yourself girl. Do not give away your position. We will deal with this in time." He whispered.

Shabakaa studied Nick and the mask. He considered trying to grab for it, but was sure a guard would take him down before he could get to it. He glared at the Egyptians and their uncivilized behavior. In his mind, he had once respected the gods for his history, now he wished them dead.

Nick looked down at Shabakaa. "Why are you staring at me boy?" Anubis demanded an answer.

"You were a respected god, once long ago on my planet. Now, you are so pathetic. You need a human to host you, to allow you to live." Shabakaa had hit the right nerve.

Anubis' eyes glowed even brighter as he approached the prisoners. "I may be a reborn version of myself, but you will respect me." With his words, he swung a fist at Shabakaa knocking him backwards across the chamber.

As Anubis walked in Shabakaa's direction, he raised a hand that was now covered in a metal bracelet, which had parts extended to his fingers. With his fingers all extended wide, a golden beam came from within. Aiming the full force of the beam at the boy, he found his target and assaulted him at a molecular level.

"Never disrespect a god. It is time you find out how powerful I really am."

Shabakaa fell flat on the floor as his body began to shake and writhe in pain. He felt himself vibrating as the beam's light coated his body. Inside Nick watched, powerless to stop the chain of events. Inside the mask, a single tear ran down his face. He knew Anubis would not stop until his friend was dead.

Thoth watched and calculated every move possible to stop the situation. Emma staired at him, impatiently waiting his help. Then Thoth raised his head and smiled. As he looked towards Emma, she could see his eyes had changed, they now looked like a computer calculating odds.

Thoth raised his hands into the sky and took control of all the electronics in the city. Then with a snap of his finger, the city went dark. Thoth watched as the beam Anubis emitted, lost power.

"What did you do?" Emma whispered.

"Quite simply my dear, I shut him down. To use the bracelet, he has to tap into the city's power grid. That is my domain. Now, he has nothing to draw from."

"Can Nick release the helmet now?"

"No, I am afraid it has its own power source. It will remain active no matter where he goes and what he does."

"We have to get it off." Emma demanded.

Inside the chamber, temporary lighting was turned on. Shabakaa lay on the ground struggling to move as the professor looked on in disbelief. There was nothing he could do to save himself or the others.

"I wish we had never gone to Egypt to the dig." He whispered.

"I am sure you do." Anubis said as his blue glowing eyes lit up his mask.

"Find out what just happened." Cleopatra ordered a guard.

As the guard approached the door, he turned to see Thoth. Without as much as a motion, Thoth sent a powerful wave of electricity through the guard's body, and he fell silently to the ground. Emma grabbed hold, drug him to the side and out of sight.

"We have to get in there and take the mask from Nick." Emma raged as she came face to face with Thoth.

"Very well, but if you go rushing in there, you will be captured."

"I don't know if I have any other choice. If I do nothing, Nick will be gone forever. He has to at least have a fighting chance."

Emma gathered her nerve, and put aside her fears of death. Deep inside, she wondered if this was how her counterpart died. If it was so, she was prepared to die, again.

Emma stepped into the doorway and locked her eyes on Cleopatra. As she moved inside, the queen slid to the edge of her seat. She had been in this moment before. A smile crossed her face. It had been so long since she had killed someone with her own hands.

Anubis studied Emma as she entered the room. His body shook as Nick fought for control. With no backup power to call on, Anubis had become a bit weaker. The transformation was not complete.

Cleopatra pulled a dagger from her belt, as she moved towards Emma. "I've never killed anyone twice." She laughed.

"Really, maybe today you will end up the victim, instead of the homicidal murderer." With the end of Emma's words, the two raced towards each other.

Chapter Twenty: Reunion

Anubis moved closer to the fight, he found it entertaining that these women would battle for his attention. As his eyes glowed as bright as ever, the mask hid a devious smile. With every moment, his control grew stronger. Anubis knew he was about to cross the line of no return. His life force would control this body forever.

Cleopatra stabbed at Emma as the two crashed into each other. The blade ran along the outer edge of Emma's shirt, ripping at her flesh as a line of blood flew forward.

Cleopatra looked into Emma's eyes; she was thrilled by the fight. The fact she drew first blood excited her. As the two continued their blows at each other, Cleopatra remembered the older version of Emma, who had died there many years ago. She was not as much of a fight as the younger version before her now. She thought this version was more sporting.

As Cleopatra lunged at Emma with her blade once more, Emma kicked forward and drove the knife from her hand. Cleopatra looked on in anger, as she had been bested by a mortal.

"What's the matter queeny? Not as good as you used to be?" Emma taunted her.

"I am good enough to kill you. After all, I have done it before."

Emma raised her eyes, as she thought about the words. She could not have been any angrier. Today she would not just fight for herself, but also for the spirit of her older counterpart, who died so unfairly.

As Emma looked over Cleopatra's shoulder, she saw Anubis standing and watching. He was enjoying himself. Emma shook her head as she scanned the room. Just to her left on the floor was a shield, left by the guard that Thoth took out. She had a weapon, she only had to acquire it.

While Cleopatra scrambled to reclaim her knife, Emma rolled to the ground and grabbed the shield. She was filled with excitement as she grabbed hold. Cleopatra spun around with the knife, just as the shield blocked its path from Emma.

"I have had just about enough of you." Cleopatra spoke, spitting blood from her lip that Emma had just slammed.

"Oh, I don't know, I am kind of enjoying this." Emma laughed.

Thoth entered the room behind Cleopatra, and nodded to Emma. He knew what she was doing, and he approved. As Emma slammed into Cleopatra knocking her down, she watched Anubis. Before Emma was blocked again, she sent the shield flying through the air.

"Stupid girl. You missed." Cleopatra snarled at her.

"Not really, I hit exactly what I was aiming for."

Cleopatra turned to look as Anubis fell forward. His mask flew to the ground and revealed a crack down the left side of his face. Nick stood staring. A look of confusion covered his face. Emma looked into his eyes which glowed blue like Anubis' mask.

He turned walking towards Cleopatra and Emma. His looks were diabolical, as he stopped just in front of them. He looked up at Emma, and she saw lines of data running across the blue in his eyes. She had seen something similar with Thoth.

She could not believe Anubis was in control. Nick still had to be in there. He had to be able to come back. For a moment she felt guilty for all that had happened between them. Then her anger returned.

"Nick, you have to fight. Come back to us. This is your only chance."

"You have lost. Give up the fight. Better yet, I am willing allow Anubis to finish this. He handles the afterlife. Maybe it would do him good to initiate the process he governs."

An echoed scratchy voice came from his throat as Anubis extended his hand. "I should be the one to finish this."

"Make it hurt, Anubis. It is time you showed what you are made of." Cleopatra allowed her psychopathic side to emerge.

As his hand raised, he touched Emma's cheek, before turning to Cleopatra. Emma smiled as she saw his eyes changing. She knew what it all meant.

Emma stood in a defensive posture as she spoke. "Make it hurt, Nick."

Cleopatra gasped as she realized what was happening. Nick's hands were around her throat as she tried to escape. The guards came, but Thoth held them back. This day, he would allow revenge on the one who killed so many.

Nick walked away as Cleopatra fell to the ground. She was spared, but badly injured. Nick turned to Emma. He had seen how she fought for him.

"Did you miss me?" He asked.

"You don't know how much." She said laughing.

Shabakaa and the professor joined them, as Nick looked over at Thoth. He had a look of approval on his face. For once, Thoth was glad he came out to experience the people of this planet.

"You said we could leave here." Nick asked.

"Yes." Thoth replied. "You had the ability all long."

"Funny, you remind me of the Wizard of OZ." Nick laughed.

"Hmm, I can see how you would think that." Thoth was amused. I am pleased you survived Cleopatra's curse. She left the gate open on your Earth as a type of revenge for those who forced her off her throne. When you return home, the gate needs to be destroyed."

"Isn't there any way it could be used for good?" Emma tried to see some value in it.

"I don't see how it could. You have no working knowledge of the device and if you did, you would still encounter far worse things in the multiverse."

"What do you mean?" The professor asked.

"Simply, if you can come here, then someone out there, could come through your gate as well." Thoth looked away.

"You know something, you are not telling us." Nick wanted the while story.

"The Replicants followed you on your journey here. As you were leaving the last world, they locked onto your signal. They had not paid that world any attention in years. Then you revived its technology and sent a beacon out across the multiverse of gates."

"We didn't know." Nick's voice cracked as he said the words.

"It means nothing now. Look to the sky."

As they looked to the north, a fleet of ships approached. They were geometric in design and looked like manmade small pieces had collected together to make one whole piece.

Above the Egyptian ships took to the sky as the Replicants fleet surrounded them. Thoth watched as the scene unfolded. There was little they could do, the Replicants were all powerful.

A voice came from above, echoed by all the ships that had taken positions around the city. Their message echoed for everyone to hear. "We are the Replicants. We have noticed your advanced technology and wish to add it to our own. Do not resist, or you will be destroyed. Defiance is unacceptable. Surrender yourself unto us."

Thoth turned to the group. "Perhaps today is a good day to die."

Chapter Twenty-One: Challenge of the Gods

From the ships floating above, the Replicants began appearing on the ground, out of beams of light. As they walked forward, Thoth studied them. Cocking his head sideways, he was amused by their design.

"Yes, human, but not human. Part machine, but not whole machine. They have implanted mechanical parts in their bodies. This is fascinating. How could they live like that?" Thoth was excited at the concept.

"You built mini computers to revive the gods. It's really not that different." Emma jabbed at him.

"No, this is very different. They are absorbing other cultures and people into their own. I have never seen such a dangerous race in person."

"Uhh, about that." Nick looked hard at him.

"Yes, I am aware, I have no body. I am still a living being in hologram form."

"Well, that is good for you, they won't be able to take you." The professor shook his head.

"Perhaps they could. If they are seeking technology, they could always find my main computer." Thoth looked scared as he transported himself back to his chamber.

In front of him, two Replicants stood studying his mechanical form. As he approached, they did not acknowledge him. They were not there for conversation; it was his advanced computer system they wanted.

As the one reached in to remove a part of his processor, Thoth split into multiples of himself and attacked. For a brief amount of time, he solidified his form and had form. His victory was a short lived one, as new Replicants appeared to take the place of those who he destroyed.

Thoth erected a shield around his processor and headed back to the city square where he found the others still watching the children of the gods, being rounded up and frozen in place to be absorbed.

Thoth called out mentally to the gods. One by one they assembled. Around them, their children stood frozen. They attacked in unison, knocking the Replicants ships from the sky.

Ra came forward, he was growing weary of the creatures. Holding his arms out wide, he called upon the sun as he turned his power against their enemies. His power was great, the Replicants were unyielding.

Nick walked forward, as the others watched. He looked around at the enemy and studied them. As he blinked his eyes, a familiar blue light returned. A data stream filled his vision as he looked for a weakness.

Nick turned loose the power he had been hiding since Anubis occupied his body. As his whole body began to glow, he aimed his light at the invaders one by one. His voice projected outwards as he locked onto each Replicant.

"I see your heart is heavy in your time of death. I will help you deal with your pain, as I cross you over to the afterlife. I will guide you."

As Nick's body began to spin around, he was lifted into the air as he sought out the lives he chose to escort into the afterlife. His reach covered the whole city. As the Replicants tried to flee, he claimed many of their invasion fleet.

Drifting back to the sand, Nick fell onto his side. Thoth moved in his direction, as he studied Nick to see if he was still alive. A groan came from deep inside Nick as Thoth shook his head.

"He is alive and still very much himself."

"How did he do that without the mask." The professor asked.

"I am not one to admit ignorance. But in this case, I do not know. Perhaps there was still some lingering energy trapped within.

"Let's hope that was all it was." Emma said as she pulled Nick's head into her lap.

She looked down at his face, as he opened his eyes. There was no blue glow. He looked up to her and smiled. His body was exhausted, but his mind was free.

"Can we go home already?" He asked trying to raise his head.

"Rest, you have earned it. I will have you moved back to my chamber, where you and your friends will be safe until I locate your gate coordinates." Thoth said as multiple versions of himself arrived to take Nick away and care for the wounded children of the gods.

"I see why Inak was so scared of the Replicants. His people did not have gods to defend them." The professor commented.

"I am scared professor." Shabakaa added.

"Why, I would think you were feeling good to have survived all you have been through in the last few days."

"I do feel fortunate, but if the Replicants can come here and do what they tried to do. Who is to say they cannot go elsewhere in the multiverse? What if they find their way to our Earth?"

"Sadly, they could, and they could do damage. But, if we make it home, we will be there to warn our people. We have an advantage now, we have knowledge." The professor said smiling.

"I guess you re right. Now, we just have to find our way home." Shabakaa pushed down his fears. For now, all he wanted was to see his family and friends again. He was willing to put his faith in Thoth's abilities.

Chapter Twenty-Two: Gateway to Home

"Your journey is done now. It is time for you to go home. You have earned that much." Thoth spoke as he led the travelers to the obelisk.

"I never thought a gateway could look so good." The professor replied.

Emma trailed behind with Nick, as the others reached the gate. She stopped and took his hand. She smiled as he turned to look her in the face. He felt more like himself, there was no longer a struggle to keep Anubis at bay.

"I am glad I got to know more of you during this adventure." Emma said as she held tight to him.

"Oh, so we are calling this an adventure?" He laughed, almost choking on the words.

"Yeah, I think adventure is so much nicer than what really happened."

"You know, when we step back through the gate and go back home, nothing will ever be the same again." Nick said looking out across the sand.

"Do we tell people?"

"No way. Besides, who would believe us?"

As they caught up with the group, Thoth turned to look at them. He was never one for attachments, but these people, he liked. He felt a kind of sadness to see them leave. He was sure he would never see them again.

"Today, you have Thoth's respect. You have taught me much, with my vast array of experience and wisdom, that is saying something. I look forward to remembering you."

"We'll remember you too. It's not every day you meet a hologram of a god from ancient Egypt." Shabakaa said laughing.

"You found our way home?" Emma asked.

"Yes, it took some time and research of the gate system. I did find your planet, which was not easy, being there were discrepancies in the records. It is all set to go. Nick, you just have to use your red crystal and activate it."

Nick moved to the edge of the table and pulled the crystal from his pocket. Placing it on the table, the other crystals all began to glow. As the group moved back a few steps, the wormhole began to form.

As Nick and the others said goodbye, they moved towards the opening one by one. Thoth looked on as the travelers walked through the gate and they disappeared into the swirl of bright color. And then, they were gone and Thoth turned away.

In an ice covered cave a few minutes later an obelisk much like the one they came through began to light up and then formed the end of a wormhole. As the travelers came flying through and landed on the ground, Nick stood up and looked around.

"Where the hell are we?" He asked as if he would get an answer.

"It appears, Thoth made a mistake." The professor replied.

"I don't understand, he said he found our planet. This is not the tomb we left from." Emma said as she shivered from the cold.

"It must me in the minus numbers here. We will freeze to death." Shabakaa shook as he tried to get the words out.

"I agree. I am going to look out the front of the cave, but if I see nothing in sight, we will have to leave or we will freeze to death."

Nick looked out into the snow squall that beat against the opening of the cave. The freezing blasts hurt his eyes and stung his face. They had no choice; they had to leave and fast.

Returning to the others, he held up the crystal and shook his head. He hoped they would do better on their next gate. Nick's hand shook as he put the crystal into place. He had a numbness starting in his fingers.

As the gate lit up and the familiar wormhole formed in front of them, for once it was a welcome sight. They wasted no time going through the gate. As their forms disappeared, the gate powered down and went into its dormant state.

Minutes later, outside the cave, the roar of a jet plane flew past. Coming in closer, it flew circles around the location. "This is Arctic Echo 1542; I located an energy source in the area of Mt. Gunnbjörn. It just appeared and disappeared a few minutes later. I don't know how to explain it. This storm is getting pretty bad, I will have to return to base. When the weather breaks, we will be able to investigate this further. If there was life here, it is gone now."

The story continues in Nick Grainer Book 2 The Quest for Atlantis

Thanks for choosing this book, if you enjoyed it,
please leave positive feedback.

**Included at the end of this book, are the first two
chapters of G.W. Mullins' Best-Selling title
Rise Of The Dark Lighter Book One –
Dark Awakening**

Daniel walked
in the land of
the dead.
Now the dead
want him
back!
For Information About
From The Dead
Of Night
The Book Series Visit
gwmullins.wixsite.com/books

About the Author

G.W. Mullins is an Author, Photographer, and Entrepreneur of Native American / Cherokee descent. He has been a published author for over 10 years. His writing has focused on the paranormal and Native American studies. Mullins has released several books on the history/stories/fables of the Native American Indians.

Among his books are the extremely successful *Star People, Sky Gods, And Other Tales Of The Native American Indians*, *The Native American Story Book - Stories Of The American Indians For Children Volumes 1-5*, *The Native American Cookbook*, and *Walking With Spirits Native American Myths, Legends, And Folklore Volumes 1 Thru 6*.

He has released the complete series from his Sci/fi Fantasy Series *From The Dead Of Night*, including the Best-Selling titles - *Daniel Is Waiting*, and *Daniel Returns*.

His most recent work includes the new series *Rise Of The Snow Queen* featuring *Book One The Polar Bear King*, and *Book Two The War Of The Witches*. He has also released *Messages from The Other Side* a nonfiction book about communication with the dead.

For further information, on his writing, visit G.W. Mullins' web site at ***http://gwmullins.wix.com/books***.

Rise Of The Dark-Lighter Book One
Dark Awakening
Is Available in Hardback (978-1-64871-256-2),
Paperback (978-1-64871-159-6) and various eBook
formats worldwide.

Nuestra Señora de la Santa Muerte, also known as Santa Muerte, is an idol, female deity or folk saint in Mexican and Mexican-American Catholicism. The personification of death, she is believed to be associated with healing, protection, and delivering her devotees safely into the afterlife. Many consider her an angel of death.

Before

The lightning struck around them, as Malachi struggled to steer the car through the debris that the storm threw in their way. His heart raced and he could feel the pounding in his chest. He was scared, probably more scared than he had ever been before. For once in his self-absorbed life, this was not about him, a life was on the line.

"Hang on Uncle, I am doing my best to get us to the hospital. The storm is not making this easy." Malachi tried to comfort him.

"I know, I am holding on. You know I never said how proud I am of you." Carl's voice trailed off into a cough.

"Be still Uncle. There will be time for that after I get you to the hospital."

As Malachi spoke, he attempted to wipe the condensation from the windshield of the car. His efforts were in vain, as he would finish wiping, the fogginess would return. The car was old and barely drivable, it should not have been on the road, but in this situation, he had no choice.

As Malachi looked away to slap his hand against the defroster, he took his eyes off the road. It was then the storm took its vengeance and a funnel cloud passed in front of them. As its winds ripped through the road, a huge oak tree began to sway. Malachi looked up just in time to see it uprooted and flying towards the car.

Malachi let out a scream, as he knew there was nothing he could do to get out of the tree's path. As the tree hit the front grill of the car, it spun out of control and rolled down the deserted street. Flipping end over end, the crushed vehicle landed at the white picket fence that surrounded a country church.

As he looked out through the broken windshield, Malachi felt the blood running down his forehead. Struggling to lift his arm to his head, he felt the pain of being thrown around the vehicle in the crash. He was not sure, but the pain in his chest felt like a cracked rib. The pain came in jabs with his every movement. At first, he did not think of his uncle, then the realization hit him, he was not hearing any noise from the back seat.

Malachi turned to look around. A feeling of dread washed over him. How could his uncle have survived? The man was at death's door before the crash. Looking to the backseat, there was nothing. He was alone in the car.

Looking up through the broken glass, he scanned the road, until he found the form of a body laying several feet behind. His heart sank as he assumed the worst. He had failed with is most important thing he had ever had to do. Pushing against the seat, Malachi attempted to move his battered body to the driver's side door. He pulled the handle and leaned in, but the door was bent and mangled.

Leaning back, Malachi pulled his legs to his chest. He felt the surge of pain as he tried to hold them back with his arms. With all the energy he could muster, he let loose and kicked the door. It flew open quickly, and with such a force, that it slammed into the fender and then to the ground.

Malachi crawled out of the opening and fell to his knees. His head spun around, as dizziness overtook him. The rain blasted all around, as he tried to look towards his uncle. With every drop that hit his head, the blood that covered him splattered and ran down his face. It was no time, before his entire face was covered in red. His eyes stung and burned as he tried to focus, and began to try to get to his feet.

He wobbled back and forth, and lost his footing, falling to the ground as soon as he stood up. He was determined. His mind raced and his life flashed before him. He had accomplished nothing in the twenty years he had been alive. His past was a blur of selfishness and a desire to acquire money.

As he slammed into the paved road, his parent's faces ran through his mind. He wondered if they would have been ashamed of him. He never considered it before. They died when he was very young. He barely knew them. It was then his uncle Carl came and took him in. Malachi felt tears welling in his burning eyes, as he realized the only person on earth that cared for him, was just a few feet away and dying.

Malachi pushed his hands onto the pavement and forced himself upwards. Crawling at first, he finally got his footing and made his way to the lifeless body he saw before him. He fell to his knees at Carl's side and screamed out.

"Be still young one, I am not dead yet." A quiet shaky voice came from Carl's lips.

"Uncle, you are alive. I thought you were…"

"Dead…you can say the word. We all must die sometime, just not this minute. Perhaps soon though." Carl began to cough with his last words.

"No, I will get you help. I promise you I will."

"Malachi, just calm yourself. Go to the church and see if anyone is there. If the priest is in, get him to come and bring me inside."

Malachi rose to his feet, and moved as quickly as he could, to the church doors. As he pulled at the handles, the doors did not move. They were locked. Malachi knew he had to find a way to get his uncle out of the storm. He drew back his fists and threw them at the red wooden door. He screamed out, as he beat on the wood, and threw himself against it trying to force his way in. Just as he was about to give up, the door opened.

"What is happening here?" Father Timothy said hastily as he looked down and saw the bloody face of Malachi. "What has happened to you my boy?"

"The storm, it caused the car to crash and my uncle is badly hurt."

"Why would you come out in a mess like this anyway?" The priest asked.

"My uncle was ill before we left, I think he is dying. Please, can you help him?"

The two made their way to Carl, who was passing in and out of consciousness. Father Timothy took hold of him, and Malachi assisted as they lifted Carl from the ground. The rain pounded down heavily upon them, as they made their way to the door of the church.

Safely inside, they laid Carl's limp body on a pew, near the front of the chapel. Carl's lips moved as if he was speaking to someone. Malachi was not sure of who, he was not sure he wanted to know. He was only sure he was more scared than he had ever been. He looked down at his hands, as they shook uncontrollably. He tried not to succumb to his fears.

The priest returned with towels and a cup of hot tea. As he reached down to Malachi, the boy just looked up to him, barely able to form words. Taking the drink, Malachi held it in his hands, warming them as the priest began to wipe the blood from his forehead and face. Malachi smiled at him trying to find the strength to say thank-you.

"Your uncle needs help that I cannot provide. I can take care of the spiritual end, but honestly, that will not save him. He needs a doctor and medicine. From the looks of him, he was having a heart attack, long before you came out into the storm." Father Timothy said as he continued to clean Malachi's wounds.

"How do we get a doctor? The storm is worse than before. I cannot go anywhere without a car." The boy said, as he hung his head.

"You cannot go anywhere regardless, you are injured. The storm is no place for you in your condition. I will go. I know the roads, and a few shortcuts."

"But how will you get there? You can't walk in this storm."

"I have a motorcycle. It was donated to the church years ago. and I have become very good at riding it. Don't look at me like that, I might be a priest, but I can do normal things you know. Stay here and watch over your uncle. I will be back as soon as I can."

"Father, please be careful. Oh, and thank-you for what you are about to do."

Timothy acknowledged him, and turned to go. Malachi admired his bravery. He wished he was braver than he was. He returned to his uncle's side looking down at him. Carl was still moving his mouth as if he were speaking. The words were not intelligible, but still he spoke under his breath.

As Malachi watched, his uncle's eyes flew open and he pulled his arms close to his chest. Calling out, his voice began to make sense, and his words were clearer. He looked to Malachi and stretched out an arm to grab at him.

Malachi went down on his knees and took his uncle's hand. "What is it uncle. Are you feeling better?"

"No, my boy, I am fighting. The demons of death are coming for me. I need help to fight them. I need you to pray for me. Pray to Santa Muerte, ask her to help me. She will come."

"Uncle, she is not real, she is only a myth. Old Spanish women prey to her as a way to escape their unhappiness." Malachi insisted.

"She is not a myth, she is real. I have known many who have seen her, she comes when life is about to end. She can save me. Please do this for me. You must give her an offering. Place a bowl of water at the alter and pray to her."

"I do not believe in this or in religion, but if it will calm you, I will do it. Now rest as I go find water."

As Malachi searched through the building, he found the kitchen and a bowl for the water. As he filled it, he shook his head, not believing he was about to participate in this craziness. In his heart he knew he had to do it, if for no other reason, to calm his uncle until help came.

Malachi returned to the chapel and placed the water near a statue and cross, in the front of the room. As he kneeled on the floor, he looked up at the Virgin Mary. He wished he believed, in this religion, or in anything that would help them. His heart was too cold and barren he thought.

As he bowed his head, he began to ask for help from Santa Muerte. He asked her to come to him, to aid him in the saving of his uncle. He offered her the bowl of water as an act of respect. Then he closed his eyes. He called for help, and the darkness answered back.

The light in the room faded, as a shadow came forward from the darkened back wall. The figure of a woman took shape. She had dark features and her head was bowed. As she slowly walked forward, Malachi looked up. He prepared to scream, as she raised a shriveled finger to her dried lips.

As he looked at her, he could make out her face, it was drawn and looked as if she had been dead. She retained the features of a woman, but was as much skeleton as human. Her skin looked as if it had been wrapped around bone with no real meat left to her body. Malachi was scared, and his heart raced as she slowly moved towards him.

As she came in his direction, Malachi fell backwards from the feet of the statue. He scrambled trying to get upright. A scream became trapped in his lips as he crawled to the side of his uncle.

Leaning down, Santa Muerte picked up the bowl of water. She moved it to her leathery looking lips and allowed the water to pass into her mouth. She drank until the water was gone. Then she sat the bowl back down and turned towards them.

Malachi stared at her, as she began to smile. As he looked, her appearance began to change. With every second, she became more human in appearance. Her skeletal structure became more flesh-like. Her body filled out, and her face became normal. She laughed out-loud as the transformation became complete.

"Your offering is accepted. I needed that. But why have you disturbed my sleep. It has been many years since I graced this plane. No one has called out to me in over a decade." Santa Muerte looked at him inquisitively.

"My uncle, he is ill. I fear he is dying. Please save him." Malachi pleaded with her.

Extending a hand, she reached down and touched Carl's head. She smiled at him as Carl looked back to her. A joy rushed over him as he saw that Malachi had done as he asked. Carl sat up as Santa Muerte cradled him in her arms.

"Your time to leave this plane was not meant to be as of yet." She spoke softly.

"What do you mean? Is he not dying?"

"That is not what I meant. He was not supposed to die for some time yet. His fate has changed."

"Can you save him?" Malachi pleaded for answers.

"It does not work that way ignorant boy. Life cannot just be given. It is an exchange. A life for a life. One forfeits, so another may live. For him to continue in this existence, another must take his place in death. Now that wouldn't be fair, would it boy?" She asked him.

"No, but I do not want him to die. You have to save him."

"Not everything is by your human choosing. If he is to live, then you tell me whose life to claim in his place. Would you choose that I take the life of the priest that left here unselfishly trying to save another, or perhaps another innocent who does not even know you. Or perhaps, you are willing to exchange your life for his?" She laughed out hysterically, as she walked around looking at the statues in the church.

"No, this cannot be. Malachi, do not even consider her offer. If this is the only way, then I choose death. Take me now Angel of Death. I believed in you and what you stand for. I had no idea you were so cruel and heartless." Carl screamed at her.

"Heartless," she laughed. "I am here to save you, and you call me heartless. I should strike you down myself for your disrespect. I was human like you, and I know the pain of death. You lived much longer than I did. Do not whine to me about your pathetic life. If you want to live, a choice must be made."

"Is there no other way?" Malachi pleaded with her.

"Perhaps, there is. I tire of coming here to this existence to take lives. Become my apprentice, help in my work. Then in the time of one year, you can win back your freedom, if you fulfill your duties."

"You mean, I would not die, and I can come back to my life."

"As pathetic as it is. Yes, you can return, but only at a time I agree. Your Uncle will live, and may do so until his actual time of death that was ordained."

"Then I agree to your terms." Malachi choked on his words.

"No, Malachi do not let her take you. She will not honor the deal. Run from here." Carl screamed.

"It is too late old man, I have him now. The deal is struck. He is mine."

As she turned to look back at Carl, she reached out a hand and Malachi took it. As they walked towards the back hall of the church, they both faded into darkness. Carl stood up, feeling the energy flowing through him again. He was healed, and his life returned. Malachi was not so lucky.

Chapter 1 - Out of The Past

Santa Muerte stood looking, through her portal into the past. She thought about her new apprentice. She watched as he slept. Her mind raced to when she was still human. Moving her hand over the portal, she saw the mist change within, the images went back to the time of 1847. The Mexican-American war raged through Texas. She stared on until she saw herself.

She clung to her mother, as they made their way through the side street trying to avoid the spray of bullets. Her mother pulled her close. Fear covered her face; she had no idea how to save them. They were surrounded by the fighting.

As her mother pulled her into the shelter at the end of the house, Anna looked up to her. She did not understand what was happening. Her mother clung to her trying to quiet her cries.

"Anna…" Her mother spoke. Santa Muerte played the moment over and over again. It had been so long since she had heard her own name said, or her mother's voice saying it. Her cold heart throbbed in her chest. She wasn't supposed to feel this way anymore. She had given up feeling anything about life or people years ago. It was too much of a toll on her. When she inherited her role as an angel of death, she left so much behind.

Looking back into the past, she watched her mother as she cared for Anna who was only six. This war was no place for her. Children were supposed to be carefree and happy. She should have been playing somewhere in a field of flowers. Instead, she was facing an army of soldiers. Santa Muerte glanced down for a moment, she knew what was coming, and that much could still hurt her.

"Mi amor, I promise this is not what I planned for you in life. Please, no matter what happens, remember mama loved you so much. If I could have changed this, I would have. I just do not know how to save you or myself."

As Carlotta finished speaking, she heard the soldiers making their way down the side street. She pulled Anna close and covered her mouth. "Do not cry, do not make a sound." She whispered, as the door began to open slowly. Carlotta raised her head as she came eye to eye with the enemy she had come to fear.

"Stand up woman." He screamed at her.

"Please, I beg of you, spare my child." She cried out.

As the soldier studied her, he did not care for her or her child. He raised his rifle into the air. A smile crossed his lips, as he prepared to claim another notch for his collection of kills. The shot rang out, as Anna watched her mother fall sideways on the ground.

Anna screamed and grabbed at her mother. She pulled at Carlotta's hand, but she did not move. Anna struggled to arouse her mother, it was no use, she was gone. The young girl had no concept of death or murder. In that day, she witnessed both within minutes. She stood looking at her mother and screaming, as the soldier reloaded his rifle.

"Looks like my lucky day, two Mexicans at the same time. Don't worry, it will be over soon." He said laughing at Anna.

She stood there watching, paralyzed by her own fear. Santa Muerte yelled at her, "Why don't you run and hide. Just save yourself." She raised her hands to her head, as the sound of the rifle firing, rang through the room. Clutching her chest, she caressed the point where the bullet had hit her. If she still had a heart, she thought it would hurt.

Her eyes filled with tears as she watched. The soldier left, walking away proud of himself and his deeds. She felt hatred filling her. She grinned, and thought to herself, there must still be some emotions left inside somewhere. As the killer turned to leave the alley, a Mexican soldier came from around the corner and fired before he was seen. The murderer fell to the ground, a grim look on his face. As he looked up, he saw the dark one coming for him.

A few feet away, the dark shadow came. As it moved forward, it took shape. A man emerged from within the darkness. Dressed in black from head to toe, he wore a dress suit and looked like an undertaker. Looking about, the dark one studied the area. "So many dead, so many souls to claim. I'll be here a while." The Angel of Death was pleased.

He cleared the street of the dead before surveying the area. He made his way down the street until finding the bodies of Carlotta and Anna. Looking down at Anna, he shook his head. "Little One, you never had a chance in life, did you?"

As he lifted Anna into his arms, he carried her through the streets. His pain was obvious, as he struck out at those who caused the death of such a young girl. In moments, he killed all who were in the immediate area, before lifting himself upwards with the child still in his arms.

In his own realm, he took Anna to his private chamber. There he took a small amount of his power and formed a ball of energy in front of him. Looking down at the girl, he aimed his hand, shooting the power within her. "My child, forgive me for what I do, but this is the only way I know to give you life again." With the power surging through her, she took a deep breath, and sat up coughing.

"Arise Muerte. My child, born of death."

"My name is Anna, she said staring at him."

"You were Anna, now you are so much more. You are Queen of the Dead."

"I don't understand." She questioned him.

"In time, it will all make sense to you. But for now, you will grow and learn."

As his words echoed through the room, Malachi watched from behind. He had been watching the whole time. He understood a little better what was happening. He had enlisted his soul with that of the dead.

Nick Grainger And The Curse Of Cleopatra

<u>Also Available From G.W. Mullins</u>

Dream Walker Book One Rise Of The SandMan

Rise Of The Snow Queen Book Two The War Of
The Witches

Daniel Awakens A Ghost Story Begins– From The
Dead Of Night Prequel

Daniel Is Waiting A Ghost Story – From The Dead
Of Night Book One

Daniel Returns A Ghost Story - From The Dead Of
Night Book Two

Daniel's Fate A Ghost Story Ends - From The Dead
Of Night Book Four

Rise Of The Snow Queen Book One The Polar Bear
King

Messages From The Other Side Stories of the Dead,
Their Communication, and Unfinished Business

Vengeance

Mullins

Mysteries Of The Unseen World – Ghost, Hauntings
and The Unexplained

Haunted America Stories Of Ghost, Hauntings And
The Unexplained

Timeless – A Paranormal Romance Murder Mystery

Star People, Sky Gods, And Other Tales Of The
Native American Indians

More Star People, Sky Gods, And Other Paranormal
Tales Of The Native American Indians

Lost Tales Of The Native American Indians Vol 1

Walking With Spirits Native American Myths,
Legends, And Folklore Volumes One Thru Six

The Native American Cookbook

Native American Cooking - An Indian Cookbook
With Legends And Folklore

The Native American Story Book - Stories Of The
American Indians For Children
Volumes One Thru Five

Nick Grainger And The Curse Of Cleopatra

The Best Native American Stories For Children

Cherokee A Collection of American Indian Legends, Stories And Fables

Creation Myths - Tales Of The Native American Indians

Strange Tales Of The Native American Indians

Spirit Quest - Stories Of The Native American Indians

Animal Tales Of The Native American Indians

Medicine Man - Shamanism, Natural Healing, Remedies And Stories Of The Native American Indians

Native American Legends: Stories Of The Hopi Indians Volumes One and Two

Totem Animals Of The Native Americans

The Best Native American Myths, Legends And Folklore Volumes One Thru Three

Mullins

Ghosts, Spirits And The Afterlife In Native American
Indian Mythology And Folklore

War Song: Tales Of The Native American Indians

Origin Tales Of The Native American

www.ingramcontent.com/pod-product-compliance
Lightning Source LLC
Chambersburg PA
CBHW071436200726
48294CB00002B/662